ALL THE WAY TO THE MOON

ALL THE WAY TO THE MOON

by ROSE TITUS

Part Three of *The Vampire Next Door* Series

All the Way to the Moon

Edited by Kelly Novak
Hypothesis Press
Andover, MA
www.HypothesisPress.com

Cover design by BetiBup33 design studio
https://thebookcoverdesigner.com/designers/betibup33/

Title page photo is of Danvers State Hospital c. 1893. ©

ISBN-13: 978-1-948785-01-3
ISBN-10: 1-948785-01-3

All the Way to the Moon

T HE SHE-WOLF padded softly through the dark forest as the snow began to gently fall. Soon the seasons would change, like they had every year since the beginning of time. She heard a rabbit off in a distance, but she had no interest in it. She ignored the rabbit and continued on until stopping at the top of a hill to look down.

There below was a small town, and she could see the glow of the few lights that were still on late at night. It was a small town off the highway, mostly surrounded by field and forest. Maybe there would be food, and a safe place to sleep. She had been running for a long time; she was fatigued since her escape and wanted to finally stop, to find a place to stay for a while.

She raised her nose to the sky and let out a long and lonely wail into the cold wind; a pack of coyotes answered her back. She went silent and continued her run through the snow.

The coyotes continued their song into the night.

Sharona woke up in the back seat of the old gray Chevy where she had been sleeping. She looked at her watch and saw it was nearly dawn. On the car's rear window she could see a light dusting of snow, but was kept warm by the wolf pelt wrapped around her, as it always was when she journeyed outside of herself.

She had begun to learn the old ways when she was very young; the pelt was given to her by her grandfather. He knew his time was coming to an end, and he wouldn't need it anymore. What he didn't foresee was the coming destruction. She was the last one left that she knew of; the last of a long line that kept secrets long forgotten by history.

Sharona startled when there was a tapping on the car's window. She unlocked the door and slowly opened it, and looked up to see a policeman.

"Is there a problem, officer?"

"Everything okay, miss?"

She cleared her throat, "Sure, fine. Everything is okay. I was driving. I got real tired. I didn't want to fall asleep at the wheel and crash, so I pulled off the road."

"Well, it's not safe to be out here alone, miss. You'd be better off to stay at a motel. There's one up the road a bit."

"Okay, thank you, officer."

"Say, that's a nice fur you have there."

"Thank you. It keeps me warm, I guess."

"You just passing through?"

"Well, I don't know. I might look around town, see if there are any jobs, or something."

He next asked her name and she gave it, "Sharona Thiessen."

"Well," he continued, "I just happen to know a place that might have an opening for a waitress, if you're interested. But you just can't park your car out here in the woods off the side of the road; it's not safe. I'm going to have to ask you to move along or stay at the motel. If you want I can ask about the job for you. If you're still in town the next few nights you can leave a message for me at the police station, and I'll make a phone call about it and find out. Ask for me, Sergeant Stepanek."

"Oh, that's real nice of you, officer."

"Kid," he said, looking straight at her, "you look like you need a little help. Can't help but notice. Everything okay?"

"Yeah, I'm okay." He was right. She didn't want to admit it, but she did need help. She needed a place to stay, and for that, she needed a job, "You're right, sir. Maybe I do need a little help right now. I'll go to the motel. I hope it's cheap."

"It is. Just pull your car out and head down that way about four miles."

Karl Stepanek drove away, wondering about the girl. He had seen many transients and runaways come through in his long time as a small town cop, but this one seemed different. Most people that were drifting through looked half drugged or otherwise out of it. This girl was wholesome looking, with blue eyes, blonde curls, and clean clothes. She didn't look like trouble. Instead, she looked like she had been in trouble. Maybe she was running away from trouble?

He could have asked to see her license, but he didn't bother. She would either find her way to the motel, or move along. If she stayed in town for any amount of time, he would check into it. He would also ask about the job, if she did stay around. Before she drove away, he did get her plate number. He could look her up that way.

He also wondered about the gray shadow of a wolf—or was it a coyote?—that he saw drifting quietly about just beyond the trees near where the girl's car was parked. He went over to look, but did not see any paw prints in the snow.

He looked up through the police cruiser's windshield. It would take longer for the sky to brighten because of the thick dark clouds and light snow beginning to dust the roadway. He would let the day shift know to keep an eye out for her. And he would remind himself to ask a few questions if and when he was able to do so.

And on the other side of the continent, almost a different world . . .

The night was only slightly cool, and the sky was clear. It was going to be a beautiful night for the art exhibit at the small local museum.

They appeared to be an unlikely couple. She wore a silk dress, Italian kidskin heels, and fine pearls; he wore faded black jeans with slightly scuffed short black leather boots, a gray t-shirt and an old leather jacket. But he was an artist, and he was expected to dress like he did not care that everyone who was someone would probably show up at the exhibit. And in fact, he did not care. He knew that the mayor along with representatives from this cultural organization and that charity group may show up, but they would be there only for a photo opportunity. He was there because it was his work on display, and he didn't care if important people shook his hand or not.

And no one in the crowd that was about to gather would know the truth about either of them: that she was the missing and presumed dead daughter of a notoriously corrupt billionaire.

And he was a vampire.

How they met was not something she was proud of. In fact, she would rather forget how they met. Laura had run away from home and found herself unable to cope with the harsh realities of living a normal life. Soon after finding a job she almost could not handle and a place to live, she discovered the existence of vampires near her new home. That fact did not really bother her much after surviving life with her father. But life in the real world caused her such distress she decided she should end it all. Being afraid to do it herself, she attempted to enlist a vampire to simply do it for her.

Instead of going along with her plan, Rick simply set her straight about a few things. But neither of them expected to fall in love.

Before they set out for the evening she asked if maybe he should wear a suit.

"What?"

She then realized he probably didn't even own a suit, and sighed, "Well, the mayor might show up."

He smiled slightly when she mentioned the mayor, and she knew he was about to launch into his usual sarcasm, "I didn't vote for that smelly, overweight and overpaid skirt chasing useless drunk."

"Never mind."

That was one of the things Laura admired about Rick; he didn't really care very much what other people thought about him. If other people wore gowns and tuxedoes he would probably put on a clean shirt and newer jeans and shine his boots and that was that. Her father, who cared so much about appearances, would hate him for that alone. She just hoped no one that she knew from her past would show up and recognize her.

After all, she was supposed to be dead.

Even if she couldn't do away with herself, her father decided to publicly declare her dead anyway.

Later that evening she was surprised to realize that she felt comfortable mingling at the exhibit; not many people bothered to speak to her beyond a few polite words. She only needed to give her first name, Laura, and introduce herself as, simply, "Rick's friend." They were more than friends, but that was no one's business.

But then she turned to see the photographer for the local newspaper. She turned her face away, and pretended to be reaching for the tray of champagne as a waitress walked by with it.

But it was too late. The camera flashed. Her face would be in print the next day.

"Don't worry yourself too much about it," Rick said as he drove her home in his '68 Catalina, "It's only a local paper. Probably only a few hundred people read it."

"I know. You're right," she sighed, and she hoped he was right.

On more than one occasion Rick had suggested she might put some of her own artwork on display. That was one of the few things they had in common: the love of art. But no, she worried that would get her noticed. And she did not want to be noticed.

He pulled up into the parking lot behind her apartment building, "Have you thought of speaking with the reporter? The one who works for the tabloid?" And who wanted to report on the rumor that the daughter of powerful billionaire Augustus Rivers was in fact still alive, out there, somewhere. "It would be a great way to get back at dear old dad." She would get paid for the interview also. The amount of money she took with her when she made her escape would not last forever.

"I just don't feel safe about that."

"I'll tell him, then."

"I would love to get back at my father, but, then again, I just don't want him back in my life. If I talked, he could find me. You don't know how vindictive he can be, Rick."

"All right, then," he said. "I'll tell him to go back to looking for Elvis and the Bigfoot."

She got out and he turned his car around and headed for home.

When he got in after midnight, there were messages on his answering machine. He looked to see Rufus in front of the television, "Aren't you supposed to be studying to finish your high school diploma?" Several months ago Rick had taken in three homeless kids to keep them from being killed on the streets. Charlie got busted for selling drugs. Jimmy was in rehab to get off drugs. And Rufus remained camped out on Rick's couch due to the fact that he had no place else to go, and also because it was discovered that his father may have also been a vampire.

"Huh?"

6

"Never mind." He went to check the phone on the kitchen wall.

There was a message from the private detective, Martin Atkinson, who used to be a cop. No luck in finding whoever could be the father of the boy now residing on Rick's couch. And another message from Leon, Rick's unofficially adopted brother. "Rick, call me," it simply said. He knew Leon would most likely be awake. He called Leon's cell phone.

He picked up, "Rick! How was the exhibit?"

"Dull. Just self-important people floating around pretending to be interested in art and trying to impress one another. What's up?"

"Remember those people I told you about on the east coast?"

Rick certainly remembered. A story was published with a college literary magazine and was seen online. It was about vampires, but the story was so close to their own reality, they wondered if the writer might know any real vampires rather than having simply made it up. Leon wouldn't stop asking to contact them until finally a meeting was held and it was agreed that he could try and reach out to them, "Well? What about it?"

"Someone wrote back."

"Oh, well." Rick imagined a polite reply stating something like, no, you are mistaken, the story I wrote is a work of fiction, and I don't know any real vampires, and that would be that. "What did she say?"

"I got this letter in the mail. You wanna come over and see this?"

"I thought you found this girl online?"

"I did. But then I didn't want to be a creep and stalk her online. So I looked up the magazine that printed the story, because it was published by a college writing department, and wrote to her at the college, you know, her name, and care of.

Thought it would be more polite. Anyway, I got this letter back, but it's not from her."

"Well, who is it from?" he asked. While he talked on the phone he looked to see that Rufus had picked up a book again in order to at least appear to do homework.

"Someone who says she's two hundred and twenty seven years old."

A cold wind howled outside the single window that gave a view of the motel parking lot. Sharona looked outside and saw her car covered in white. It was early spring, and almost too late for snow. But at least for tonight she would have a warm bed, and more important, a bathtub. She closed the curtains, and fell into the bed, under the covers, and slept in her jeans and t-shirt, leaving her boots on the worn out carpet by the bed. She realized she probably wouldn't be able to stay there long; her money would start to run low soon. For extra warmth, the wolf pelt covered her also.

She ran her hand through the fur and a tear dropped onto the pillow. She would never forget what happened, and wondered if the sadness would ever go away. Was she truly the last of her kind? Even if she was not, there was little chance to find any others like her.

She was brought up by her grandparents. Her parents died in a car accident, but there was talk of them being run off the road. Her grandfather started teaching her when she was very young, to project her mind outside of herself, to let her spirit take the shape of an animal, to not only wander the forest at night, but to wander the spirit world, to be able to see the other side, the way people did thousands of years ago before written history began.

But then that fateful night the mob came to their small home. Some of them seemed to be drunk. The men were beating down the door, yelling that her grandfather was a damned werewolf. He handed her the fur, "Take it; it's yours now." And then he grabbed the coffee can that he kept in an upper cabinet above the kitchen sink, "and you might need this."

"No. I'm not leaving you!"

"Go out the back door now, before they go around to the back of the house."

"No!"

"Sharona," her grandmother said quietly, "don't argue. Just go. Run while you still can. We'll try to slow them down. You have your life ahead of you. We don't. You know what these men will do to you if they catch you. Now go!"

The house was burned to the ground that night. All that was left was what the men didn't destroy. Her grandmother's Chevy, the wolf pelt, and the coffee can filled with cash and the extra set of keys to the car. Everything she needed to escape was there, as if they knew. And they probably did. She knew her grandparents were in a better place, with her parents now. She remembered being told that spirits watched over the living. She hoped that it was true.

Old enough to drive, but not quite old enough to be on her own, she ended up in foster care. When the social worker brought her to the foster family, she knew immediately something was just not right. Probably it was the way the man looked at her, the man she was supposed to call "daddy." It was also unusual that all the other children in the foster home were little girls. Pretty little girls.

"If it's okay with you, I'll just call you Mr. and Mrs. Pimlott. I mean, because my real parents are dead, and all."

"Oh, no, sweetie, you're going to think of us as mommy and daddy!" Mr. Pimlott told her, with a bright smile that she suspected was artificial, "Okay, cutie?" And he pulled her close and gave her a strangely tight hug.

"Okay, I guess," she said. She kept the fur wrapped in a bag with the rest of her things, and stashed it under her bed where it wouldn't be seen.

She did not sleep the first night at the home, or the next night, or the next. Mr. Pimlott, who demanded to be called "daddy," was heard wandering up the stairs to where the girls' bedrooms were. She listened and heard a stifled cry. She knew what she had to do.

Mr. Pimlott opened the door to her room one night, "What? There's a dog in here! How'd this dog get in here?" Daddy Pimlott screamed. "It's after me!"

From that night on she sent her spirit outside of herself in the form of the wolf to sit at the top of the stairs to snarl at Daddy Pimlott each time he tried to come up to bother the other girls in the house. He called the police to complain of a vicious dog in his house. "I think it's a German shepherd! It's vicious! I don't know how it got in here! I have helpless children in this house!"

The police came and searched the house.

"It was here! Officer, I swear, there was a dog, a big snarling awful dog." He turned to Mrs. Pimlott, "Isn't that right, honey?"

"Oh, yes, it was up at the top of the stairs, staring down at us. It snarled at my husband! I don't know which one of the children let it in."

"Girls!" demanded Daddy Pimlott when the policemen finally left. "Which one of you little bitches brought that dog in here?"

None of the other children spoke. The girls were lined up in the living room, and Mr. Pimlott sat in his favorite soft chair, his wife standing by his side. "Sharona? Did you bring that damn dog in this house?"

"No, sir."

"You sure?"

"I'm sure, Mr. Pimlott."

"I told you to call me daddy!"

"Okay, daddy. No, I did not let a dog in the house, daddy." It's a wolf, you dumb pervert. But she kept to "yes, sir," and "no, sir," and kept quiet.

"If I find out which one of you girls is bringing that dog in this house, that girl is gonna wish she left that mutt at the pound."

The next day Sharona returned from school, walked through the door, and seeing Mrs. Pimlott's face, knew there was trouble again.

Mr. Pimlott came around the corner. "What the hell is this?" He held up the pelt close to her face.

"Okay, Mr. and Mrs. Daddy Pimlott. I'm a werewolf! Now give me back my fur!" She snarled, and reached to snatch it back. She put the fur over her head, so that the wolf's ears stood up and the luxurious pelt covered her back, the tail touching the floor. "That was me at the top of the stairs! And if either of you morons ever bother any of these children again, you'll wish you hadn't!"

Mrs. Pimlott screamed.

Sharona went to her room to quickly gather her few belongings.

"Are yah really going?" It was twelve year old Becky following her to her room. Behind her were thirteen year old Lucy, and ten year old Ashley.

"I have to go. I can't stand this place anymore. I'm sorry." The fur was still over her head and covering her back as she looked at them, the long gray tail touching the floor. "Look, you guys gotta tell someone what happening in this house, okay? It's not right. It's against the law, what he does. He can't do that. You girls gotta tell a grown-up, because I'm going, and I just can't protect you anymore." She picked up her suitcase, and didn't bother to take the wolf skin off her head as she headed back down the stairs.

11

"Are you, like, really a werewolf?" Ashley asked.

"Yeah, I guess that's what they call people like me. I mean, there's not many people like me. I'm probably the last one. It's not like on TV, you know. It's a lot more complicated than that."

"Really?" Lucy started to follow her down the stairs, "I don't know if I believe it. If I put that on my head, can I be a wolf, too?"

"No, sorry. It takes a long time to learn how to do this stuff. Look, I have to go, okay? And remember, tell a grown-up. But don't tell them about me. No one will believe you. They'll believe you about Mr. Pimlott, though, if you back each other up. And if they ask about me, just tell them I left for parts unknown."

Mrs. Pimlott stood out in the hallway staring at her as she headed for the door. Sharona stopped and glared back, "How the hell can you cover up for that pig?"

"He pays the bills," she answered weakly.

Sharona snarled again and slammed the door on the way out. And then she was gone. She got into her grandmother's Chevy that she had kept parked on the street in front of the Pimlott home and hit the road. She was glad she hid the coffee can full of money in the car, where Daddy and Mrs. Pimlott would never see it. She knew it wouldn't last forever, but it was enough to get her down the highway. As to where the road would lead, she did not yet know.

Sharona woke up hoping she was back home and that the past year had just been a horrible nightmare, but when she opened her eyes she saw that she was in the cheap motel. She looked down on the floor where she had left her old worn out boots and saw the coffee can was still there. It was removed from the car in case the car was towed or broken into. She would depend on its contents for food and gas until she found a job of some kind. She reached down to pick it up, and opened it. There was enough for a month, maybe, she guessed, and she could get some clean underwear, a few decent meals and a few other things. But what would happen when the money ran out? She looked down into the can when she saw something metallic at the bottom buried under the cash. She pulled it out; it was a gold locket on a chain. Opening it, she found a small photograph of her parents, probably taken just before they died.

"We hid that for you, in case they came for us."

"What?" She looked up sleepily, wondering if she were dreaming again. "Grandpa?" She sat up, suddenly seeing his translucent image hovering by the foot of the bed. She was always told that sometimes spirits could appear to the living and visit from the afterworld, but she had never before seen spirits while not in wolf form, wandering on the other side.

"Your parents are here at peace with us on this side. And though you do not see them, they watch over you."

Then slowly her grandmother also appeared. "We knew those men would eventually come, but we didn't know we would be taken from the Earth so soon. The madness that has come down through all the centuries, it never ends. You must always be careful."

"Remember everything we taught you, and know we watch over you, and even when you cannot see us, we are with you. Use the wolf to protect yourself, and to protect others. You will go where you are needed."

And they were gone, vanished. Was it a dream? She half believed that she must have been dreaming, but she knew that she wasn't.

Rick walked up the flight of stairs toward Leon's small apartment, came around the corner, and knocked on his door.

"It's open. I knew you'd come, so I left it unlocked."

Rick stepped in and saw that Leon was watching the DVD player, "This is my favorite part, when Luke sees Ben's ghost."

"Is that the hundredth time you've seen that movie?"

"No. Just the ninety-ninth." He hit pause.

"And you can quote every episode word for word, I know. Well, this thing you want to show me. Can we be sure this is not a hoax?"

"Rick, hey come on. Look, you guys exist. So why can't more people like you exist?"

"Just always thought we might be the last ones, I suppose." He sat down on Leon's worn out sofa. He did not bother to take his leather jacket off; he didn't intend to stay long.

Leon had the letter kept in the envelope it had arrived in. The return address was a post office box. "Here, read it. Someone must be old fashioned. She handwrote it in very neat penmanship."

Rick read it silently. It was addressed to Mr. Leon Ramirez Andreyev, as Leon's legal name was Leon Ramirez but he often used the name of his adoptive family. The lady who wrote it thanked him for contacting them, and asked that the letter not be shown to anyone that it did not concern. In other words, Rick guessed, to not show it to the general public. She went on to say that at the beginning of the twentieth century she led a small group away from Eastern Europe to avoid being hunted down and slaughtered. They made their way to the United States and lived quietly in a small town, keeping domesticated animals to supply blood. "Sounds like it. Yes, during that time in history, many of us left Europe, and some of us remained behind. We haven't heard from them since before the Second World War. The ones that stayed behind, they may have all been killed, too. Leon, we may have found others like us, finally. We're not the last of our kind. We should show this letter to the others, maybe tomorrow night."

"Rick. Aren't you at least excited?"

14

"I'm in shock, Leon. I didn't think we'd ever find any others out there. I thought the rest of us had been all hunted down." The letter closed with, *We would very much like to correspond with all of you, for it has been so long since we have had any word from others of our kind and have been bereft of any hope that we are not the last.* It was signed simply with *Annasophia*. No last name given, probably for privacy, and he understood that. "Well, I suppose a post office box is more secure than the web these days. We wouldn't want the powers that be reading our messages." He handed the letter back to him.

"Rick, communicating like this can take weeks. Maybe months."

"Well, if someone over there can communicate by email, we need to watch what we say, in case it's being read by people who aren't supposed to see it. I don't want the CIA and the NSA to read anything of ours, because I hear they can do that. Leon, thank you. I've got to go," he stood up. The sky was beginning to brighten. "I'll tell you what. We should write back to her. And soon." He drifted out the door, wondering how many others were out there, thinking that they might not be the last of their kind after all. And he wished he could find them and tell them, *you are not alone.* He knew they were very far away, whoever they were, in the northeast. The weather would be perhaps still cold where they were. He wondered if they were still getting snow. He wished he could be there, where they were, and meet them, to somehow reach across the thousands of miles.

He arrived home and came in to see Rufus asleep on the couch, surrounded by a pile of homework he had finally started doing. He wondered about the boy, and where he had come from. The search was on for his father, and the search had led to nowhere so far. No other vampire in the community claimed any missing son, yet here he was, flat on Rick's couch. Oh well, Rick sighed, the kid had to be somewhere; it might as well be his living room. If he went back on the street, he wouldn't last

15

long at all. He'd begin to starve for lack of blood, and possibly do something drastic. And no one wanted to see that happen.

He wandered into his small kitchen and noticed another message on his phone. It was from Laura. Martin had called her and said that someone was trying to find her. He hoped it wasn't going to turn into another problem that they didn't need. Who would be looking for her? She was supposed to be dead. Her father had made sure of that.

Laura came home from work after being worried all day. Who could be looking for her? She hoped it wasn't her father, or anyone that worked for him: those people he had sometimes hired to "take care of things." She did not want to be one of those things that "had to be taken care of." She did not know much about the darker side of her father's business dealings, but remembered seeing some unpleasant characters drive up to the mansion to meet Mr. Rivers in his private office. They were paid in cash. People who gave him difficulty sometimes disappeared. And that's all she knew. She really didn't want to know any more, but she had suspicions.

She listened to a message on her cell phone. It was from the private investigator, Martin Atkinson, who used to be a police detective but gave it up in disgust with all the corruption in the department. The message said that someone was looking for her, and had a very important message for her, someone by the name of Zelda.

"Zelda?" she said out loud. The only Zelda she knew was one of the maids she had grown up with. She was from somewhere in Eastern Europe, and had always been kind to her as a little girl, but poor Zelda didn't seem to understand a word of English.

Zelda wanted to meet her, said the message. It was important. Well how would they communicate, she wondered, unless her English had improved? She quickly called Martin back, "Hello? Martin?"

"Yes, Miss Rivers?" he answered.

"You said a lady wanted to meet me? She had something important to tell me?"

"Yes. In fact, she said if I could get you to come down to the office, she would come back to meet you here. I have her cell phone number. She came to my office a few days ago, asking if I could help find you. It's just an odd coincidence that I know you. It's also probably because there aren't many private investigators in town, I suppose. And my office is across from the hotel where she says she's staying. I didn't tell her any of that, of course. I waited to see if you wanted to meet her."

"Well, Martin, last time I saw her, she didn't speak English very well."

"She must have learned it, then, because she speaks English well enough now."

"How can I be sure it's not someone my father sent to find me? I mean, tell me, is she short, brown hair with streaks of gray, thick dark eyebrows?"

"That sounds like her. Why don't you come down? I'll have my gun in the desk if there's any trouble."

She parked her BMW behind the building where Martin's office was, hoping no one would see it. She got out of the car and pulled her large round sunglasses out of her purse, so as not to be noticed or recognized. Martin's small office was down the stairs in the lower level of the building. She didn't bother to knock. There, when she walked in, was Zelda, no longer in her maid's uniform; no, she wore blue jeans and a colorful t-shirt with sequins stitched to it in a rose petal pattern. She did not look the same as the old lady who used to shuffle around the mansion with a feather duster.

"Darling!" she stood up. "I have found you!" The old woman pulled her close in a tight embrace, "Oh how long have I wanted to see you!"

"Zelda! You learned English? I'm impressed; you speak it very well now."

"No, Laura. I always knew pretty good English. I just pretended to not know, so Mr. Rivers not yell at me like he does everyone else."

"Oh my God. Really? You knew English, all the time you worked at the mansion, and pretended to not understand?"

"Mr. Rivers is very mean man! Sit down. Now, I have important things I must tell you. Very important things."

Laura found a seat in Martin's small office, "Well, I have to know, how did you know to look for me in this town?"

"I still work for Mr. Rivers, so if you ever see him, my dear, do not tell him this. Do not tell him I came to see you. I could lose my job, or worse. I was cleaning around his office, and saw a picture of you on his desk. It was a picture of you in a newspaper. I was curious, you see, because I saw a man drive up and he had this paper in his hand when he came in. He came in with it folded up, and he was let in and he went right to see Mr. Rivers in his office. So when I was cleaning around there I saw it and I read it. There was a picture of you. I memorized the location of where you were when the picture was taken, and put it back, before anyone saw me. I don't know if they know I read, you see."

"Oh my God, that means he's found me." She looked at Martin in shock. "I knew it. They took a picture of me and Rick at the art gallery where his artwork was on exhibit that night. He told me not to worry, but I just knew something would happen."

"Wait, Laura, there is more," Zelda said. "I have always known this, but never told. You need to know. Mr. Rivers is not your real father."

"What?"

"That is right, dear. Mr. Rivers is not your father."

"Then who is my father? And how do you know he isn't my father?"

"Because, my dear, your real father was my son."

"What?" she said again. "That would mean you're my grandmother."

"That is right, darling. And that's why I needed to find you. Mr. Rivers is still thinking about you. And I have to do something to protect you. After so much that I have seen, over the years, working for that horrible man, I now am starting to believe he might have killed my son and your mother. You know your mother died in a car accident, but do you know my son was in the car with her?"

"No. All I know is she crashed her Porsche. Daddy . . . I mean, Mr. Rivers, told me she was drunk, and wrecked the Porsche that he bought for her."

"No. Your mother never drank much. And people whispered that it might not have been an accident. I wasn't sure if I believed it, but after working there and listening when they think I can't understand much, you know, now I think so. Maybe the car was, how you say it? Interfered with? Cut the brake lines, or something. I stayed there for many years to watch over you. I saw how horrible he was to you, and it broke my heart. But I stayed to keep watch over you. I hated him always; I so hated working for that man. Well, my son, he was a gardener. And Mr. Rivers was so miserable to your dear mother, of course she stopped loving him. I believe maybe she married him for the money, but then saw how he really was, and came to hate him. She was beautiful, but he treated her like he owned her. He told her what to wear, he wouldn't let her have friends, he criticized her always. She could have no opinions of her own. She fell in love with my son. The accident happened after you were born. Mr. Rivers was on a business

19

trip, but they had been fighting, he and your mother. I think he had something done to her car. You had a nanny to look after you, and so your mother and my son, they went for a drive. They never came back."

"Oh my God," Laura sat in shock, staring blankly at Martin, who looked back at her silently.

"She didn't say what it was about, Laura. Only that it was important that she speak to you," he said. "I had no idea."

"That's why I had to finally find you. I stayed working for him, many years, to look after you. Then you disappeared one day. He said you died, and said the funeral was to be private, but I saw your suitcases were gone from your room, and saw out the window a taxicab come. So I figured you had left. I decided, one day, I must find you somehow and tell you. I also decided to look for another job, but it's been a whole year and nothing. I've been looking, anyway. I am here. I have found you. I can tell the truth to you now, and warn you."

"This is all such a shock. I . . . I just don't know what to say. Can I buy you dinner? We can go somewhere, and talk some more. I don't know anything about you, really, and I feel I should know all about you. I feel like now there's an empty place in my life where my real family should be. I'm starting to understand my whole life was a lie until I went out on my own. I don't tell many people this, and I'm not proud of it, but after listening to the man I thought was my father criticize everything about me for so many years, well, there was a time I felt I wanted to take my own life. But someone talked me out of it. You should meet him. I wouldn't be here, if it wasn't for him." She stood up. "Martin, thank you."

Rufus woke up at dusk and sleepily started to remember that he was supposed to go to the library to study, or that was what he had promised to do. Deep down, he knew Rick was right. But he hated school before his life on the streets, and he figured he would probably hate it just as much now. He showered, put on the same clothes he wore last night, and went to the refrigerator to look for something. Rick had bought the usual things and left them in the refrigerator, milk, eggs, bread, and such. They were on the lower shelf. Rufus looked at the bottles on the top shelf of the refrigerator and stared. He longed for it but could not yet bring himself to consume any of it. He would have to start sometime, and soon. Solid food was beginning to make him feel ill, as Rick told him it would.

He made himself some toast with peanut butter on it and ate it; then he finally began his way out the back door, down the back steps. On his was down he looked into the backyard where Rick kept his old car and realized that the car was slightly jacked up and that Rick was under it.

"Hey, kid, c'mere."

"Huh? Me?"

"Is there any other kid besides you over there? I don't know, because I can't see much while I'm under this Pontiac."

Rufus shuffled across the grass and over toward the car. He had known Rick for several months and finally ceased to be afraid that the vampire would cause him any harm. In fact, he had slowly come to realize that Rick was the only man he had known in his young life who had not attempted to exploit him or hurt him in some way.

"Yeah?" he asked, not knowing why Rick called him over. Rick usually ignored the boy who resided on his couch during the day, as he spent most of his time working at night. Rufus gazed down at Rick's feet while the rest of him was under the car, "What's up?"

"Okay, now listen. The world's greatest detective hasn't found your real dad. And like it or not, you're not like other kids."

"I know," he mumbled sadly.

"And you have a lot to learn."

21

"I know," he repeated.

"Somebody has to teach you how things work."

"I know."

"So, hand me that oil filter wrench."

"Huh?"

"The oil filter wrench. You should be able to see well enough in the dark."

"I can see fine. I don't know what the hell it is you want."

"It's the round thing with a handle on it," Rick said.

Rufus looked around and saw what looked like a round thing with a handle on it. "This here?" He handed it to Rick.

"Thanks. Okay. We haven't found your dad, and I guess it's going to have to be up to me." Rick came out from under the car and pulled along a shallow pan full of dark oil. He then went with the filter wrench under the front of the car to remove the oil filter.

"So, like you're gonna teach me to fix cars?"

"I can teach you that, and I can teach you more important things that you need to know. Now, remove the old filter, and when you take the new filter out of the box, coat the gasket with the used oil before putting it on."

"Am I gonna have to do this?"

"No. You can pay someone else to do it when you have your own car."

"Then why do you do it?"

"Because I can. Now, Rufus pay attention. You're getting older, and there are a lot of things you need to know." He spun the new filter onto the engine and tightened it. "You probably already realize that most of what people believe about vampires is false. We do not kill people, or fly, or sleep in coffins, or any of that."

"I know," he repeated again. "So why do people believe all those stupid things?"

"Well, we do appear to be dead when we're asleep. I suppose long ago well-meaning people would have found one of us and figured that poor individual was dead, and then that poor individual could have awakened in a coffin due to being put in it while not actually being dead. Then the well-meaning people saw that person get up and get out and they all must have panicked. Now, people used to also believe we have no reflection in a mirror, because in ancient times when people looked at their reflection they thought the image in the mirror was their soul, and they also believed vampires have no souls, which of course is ridiculous. That explains that one." Rick crawled out from under the car and stood up and reached for one of several plastic bottles of motor oil and began to pour into the engine.

"So, we do have souls?"

"I can't answer theological questions, but if most people do, then I would assume we do, too."

"Do we all have cool cars?"

"No. But you can have a cool car if you grow up, get a job, and save up to buy one, or else get an old one and fix it up yourself. Now, go to the library and study like I told you to. We don't want any dummies. We can talk more later."

Sharona's feet hurt and she was tired from carrying heavy trays back and forth but she needed the job and so she tried to ignore her exhaustion. She never imagined working in a truck stop, bringing hamburgers and fried chicken to loud men that yelled at her to hurry up, but after sleeping in her car, she would take any job that was offered and try her best to keep it.

"Honey, come over here! We want more coffee!"

"Okay." She got the coffee pot and hurried over.

"Hey," whispered the other waitress. "Watch out."

"Huh?"

"Don't get too close to the table when you pour his coffee. That guy over there likes to try to grab our butts."

She tried to stifle a laugh. "Thanks. I'll watch out. What's your name again?"

"Josie."

"Thanks, Josie."

The man tried to reach over but Sharona was quick to jump out of the way and managed to not spill anything. "Enjoy your coffee, sir!"

He laughed along with the other men at the table. "Thanks, cutie pie!"

It was after midnight and their shift was nearly over. The crowd thinned out and the girls needed to clean up for the crew that would come to work when the sun came up and people started arriving for breakfast.

Sharona finished wiping down tables and Josie ran a small vacuum around the cheap carpet to pick up crumbs and other debris.

"So," Josie said, "you're not from around here, are you?"

"No. I was a foster kid." She figured it would be safe to talk because Josie seemed to be about her age. "But the guy was being a creep, so I left. I mean, I wasn't supposed to leave. But I did. I told him and his wife off and just got in my car and drove off, didn't look back. But before I did, I told the other girls they should report him to someone."

"Wow. That's awful."

"Yeah, I lived with my grandparents, but they died. Their house burned down. All I have is the car they gave me, and a few of my things," meaning the things she took with her before the house was set on fire. "I don't ever want to go back into one of those homes, not ever. I'm old enough to be on my own. I'll manage somehow."

"So, where are you staying?"

"The cheap motel that's down the road. It's a dump. I hate it. But it's better than sleeping in the Chevy, I guess. It's gonna eat up most of my paycheck, though. I'll have to find a cheaper place if I want to save for school, or something. I mean, I don't know what I want to do yet. I'll figure out a way to go to a community college, or vocational school, some day. I don't know. Right now, all I know is, I can't go back to the place where I was." She admitted it; she had no home. "I don't think I want to just get loans, because I'll be paying them forever. But I'll find a way to go to college somehow."

"Wow," Josie said again. "Hey, this girl I know, she said she wants to rent rooms in her house. It's a big old house. She inherited it, and inherited some money, too. But she wants to make some money to pay the bills so she won't use up all her savings, and stuff. I think she's trying to start a boarding house, make some money so she can keep the old house. There used to be a boarding house in town run by an old lady. But some kid who rented a room started making some drugs or something stupid like that, and he blew the place up."

"Wish I inherited some money," Sharona sighed, "I'd go to college and wouldn't have to jump out of the way when someone tries to grab my butt."

"Want me to call her for you?"

"How much is she asking to rent the room?"

"I think she said seventy five a week for a small room, a hundred for a big room. I'll call her if you want."

"You would? That would be great. I can't stand another night at that dump. I hear people fighting in the next room and some strange bug was crawling around the cheap rug. This house is clean, right?"

"Yeah, it's a little old, but it's not bad."

"Oh my God, thank you."

When Rufus returned he found Rick sitting in the living room that Rufus now considered home, sort of. He was sitting in the large, soft chair on the opposite side of the television, holding a large mug, and with his feet on the coffee table.

"Okay, kid. You might as well sit."

"You were waiting for me, right?"

"Well, yes."

Rufus sat on the couch that he slept all day on. "You look all serious."

"I suppose we have to have a serious talk. Okay, Rufus. Unfortunately, no one has been able to locate your father. If we did find him, it would naturally be his job to have this serious talk. But he is nowhere to be found. Hopefully if we keep looking, he might turn up some day."

"My mother said he didn't even know about me. She left him before I was born," Rufus recalled sadly. "So, I guess it's not like he just up and left and forgot about me on purpose."

"No. I didn't think so. Because, you see Rufus, in this community, we all look out for each other. There aren't very many of us, and for most of history people have hunted us down and slaughtered us. The most important thing is you must look out for your own kind. Every one of us, his or her duty will be to help another vampire who needs help, shelter, protection, whatever it is, within reason. This is why I don't understand why there are so many people living on the streets. You would think all societies would do the same for their own people." He took a sip from the mug. "But no, they don't."

"That's why you take care of me?" Rufus asked, and he recalled so many stepfathers who either beat him or abused him in ways he would rather not talk about or remember.

"Yes. Others in the community know about you now, and it's time to introduce you around."

"Yeah? I hope they don't think I'm a loser for being a street kid."

"I haven't told anyone what you did to survive out there, okay?"

"Okay."

"That's all in the past, Rufus. It's unfortunate, but that's the society we have to live in. Never mind . . ." Rick paused a brief moment while remembering events of a year ago. "You know, when the serial killer was still lurking around, I befriended a homeless man, took him for fast food once in a while to listen to him talk, trying to figure out what he knew about the killer. His name was Bruce; wouldn't give me his last name. One night he told me some guy took him in off the street, and he thought the guy was okay because he was a divorced dad with a kid and all that. He stayed for a while, made friends with the kid; but Bruce ran out of that house one night and went right back to the street where he felt safer, because, well, you can guess. Of course, shortly after that, he was killed. So it's not just kids who have a rough time out there. But forget all that. Here comes the important stuff. The next ten years are going to be difficult, but you will stop aging around thirty."

"Cool."

"Pay attention. You'll be able to walk in the sun until around that time, give or take a few years. You have to find a job you can do at night. You have to get your education taken care of. And you have to know the rules we live by. You can't just do whatever you want. That's another reason why I wanted you to stay here. If you stay on your own and have no one to teach you, you would end up getting hurt; or hurting someone else. And we can't let that happen."

"I won't do anything to nobody, Rick. You know I wouldn't."

"If you got hungry enough, if any of us got hungry enough, there is always the possibility of . . ." he hesitated. "Rufus, self-control is going to become very important."

"I know," he mumbled.

"Typical reply for a kid," Rick sighed. "You're going to be undergoing some changes. Do you remember being a little kid and a tooth fell out and a new one grew in? As you approach thirty, that sort of thing will happen again."

"I was kind of wondering about that. Like, if my father was supposed to be a vampire, how come I don't have sharp teeth?"

"Because you're a kid. Now, already the sun makes you uncomfortable. It's going to get worse. Solid food is making you sick to your stomach; and that will get worse, too."

"Okay. So this is not cool."

"That's why you don't have to go through this alone."

"Yeah? When do I meet everybody?"

"Not until you're done listening to my boring monologue."

Rufus rolled his eyes and exhaled.

"You are going to have to take this seriously. And I don't like having to give this talk because I don't get to make annoying jokes that you won't understand anyway. Because if you hurt any non-vampire type person, the community is going to have to kick your ass all the way to the moon."

"Yeah, okay. I get it. I have to sit through this. I'll pay attention. I don't want to be in trouble."

"Good, because some day you will thank me." Rick took another sip from his mug and continued, "Movies and trashy novels have ruined our reputation over the centuries. You see in these movies a vampire moves into a town, and bodies start turning up completely drained. A well-fed vampire would never do that, or need to do that. Going too long without blood could unfortunately lead down that road. No one wants to see anything like that happen, ever. We'd be discovered, and uneducated people would start hunting us all down."

"I won't. I swear."

"I know you won't, Rufus. But you need to know these things." He inhaled and continued on, "You are not invincible, and never will be. If you get run over by a bus, you're going to

28

be as dead as most average people after being run over by a bus."

"So, I won't step in front of a bus."

"You're immune to most diseases, and that's another reason why people have always been superstitious about us. We survived the plague that wiped out most of Europe. A lot of viruses don't affect us. And you won't live forever. Around age three hundred, you will start to age again. Most of us don't last long after that."

"So, how come people think we're supposed to be immortal?"

"Before the twentieth century, most people lived to be forty, I suppose. And most people could not read or write. If a vampire was known to be nearby, probably no one wrote down when that person came to be, or wrote down the date he faded out of existence, and people didn't live long enough to notice anything except the longer lifespan we have. And then around the beginning of the twentieth century, most people stopped believing in us, which was good, because if you don't believe in something, you're not going to hunt it down to destroy it."

"Okay," the boy interrupted. "Can I ask something? Like, why?"

"Why they want to destroy us? Simple. They watch how awful we are portrayed in movies."

"No! I mean, why do we live so long, and need to live off blood, and all that? What makes us this way?"

"That's a good question. It's genetic, you might have figured already. We've got people working in the scientific field, doing research. They work a night shift in a hospital, and in their spare time, they try and figure out the answers to those questions. We've been around for thousands of years, and for thousands of years, people have feared us. But now we have the technology to find things out. Maybe soon, we'll know more. But right now, we just don't have all the answers. All we know at this point is that our DNA is in fact quite different than that of the average person. I'm not a scientist, and I don't know enough about it myself to tell you much more than that."

Rufus stared back at him, his eyes wide, and was finally silent.

"Now here is what very few people, other than people like us, know. Your fangs will be hollow."

"Huh?"

"That's right. Like a snake's. When a poisonous snake bites, the fangs deliver venom. Then the person will die, unless they get treatment. However, we do not carry any venom. Instead, there's a drug like effect; you'd be injecting the person with a sort of substance that makes them feel high, relaxed, and all that. Very intoxicating. But that only comes about when you're in the right mood. Any other time, that wouldn't happen."

"When I'm in the right mood?"

"Yeah. You know. Like, when you like a girl. You're around her, and something in your own chemistry changes. You'll feel it, like pressure building up above your teeth. But you don't do anything about it without her consent, do you understand?"

"Huh? Oh, yeah."

"Sometimes people pass out the first few times, but they're always fine. Just remember not to drink too much. They have a harder time recovering if you do."

"Yeah, okay, like, wow, I'm really glad you told me this now."

"Oh, and don't smile too much, people might notice." Rick stood up and went to put the mug in the kitchen sink and wash it out. "I never had a kid. I was married once, but never had any kids. I had a cat once. That didn't work out too well."

"What happened to the cat?"

He drifted back out into the living room. "The cat got run over by a bus. Now if you're going to stay up late as usual, you might as well keep studying." He reached for the book bag that Rufus sometimes carried around and handed it to him.

The boy rolled his eyes, "You ain't gonna give me a break, huh?"

"You are going to become a useful and productive vampire, Rufus. If your father was around, I'm sure he'd say the same thing."

"Damn." Rufus startled when he heard a knock at the back door.

"Rick?" It was Laura, and she sounded excited. "Rick! Are you home? There's someone I want you to meet!"

"It's your girlfriend."

Rick didn't know if the boy was being sarcastic or not. "What did I say about homework?"

"Yes, sir."

This time, Rick knew Rufus was being sarcastic.

"Okay, so . . ." she hesitated, "seventy five a week is okay?"

"Yes," Sharona answered quickly. "In fact," she reached into her purse and pulled out a handful of cash. "I'll pay the first week right now."

"Really? Okay, great." The young woman who owned the big old house took the cash. "But you haven't seen the room yet."

"It's okay. It's probably better than where I am now. What's your name again?"

"Muriel," she said, "Muriel Aubrey."

"Thanks, Muriel. I just don't want to stay in that dump of a motel anymore. Roaches are crawling around on the bathroom floor. The couple in the next room are yelling all night long, too." Sharona sat down on the old wooden chair that was against the wall in the primitive kitchen. She dropped her meager belongings beside her and at her feet, the tote bags with the few items of clothing she owned, with the coffee can stashed at the bottom of one of the tote bags. She would find a place in her room to hide it later. "There was a drunken brawl in the parking lot, and the cops came to break it up. I didn't get much sleep last night. And it's way too expensive, even if it is all run down. I just gotta get out of there. I mean, really. And I just got this job. I think staying at that place will eat up most of my paycheck. This is a real nice old house, too."

"I'm glad you like it. In fact, it's a lot of work." Muriel had a broom in one hand, the cash in the other, and had been attempting to make the old place presentable before Sharona came in. "I inherited it. I can't afford to modernize it much, but I can keep things fixed and in working order, you know, like the plumbing, and stuff. There's been so many repairs lately." She didn't want to admit she was afraid to start using up the rest of the money she inherited last year. "Well, you can park your car on the street; it's a quiet neighborhood, so I don't think anything will happen to it, and . . . oh, that's a nice fur. What is that? Coyote?" Muriel saw the black and gray tail sticking out of one of the bags.

"No, it's timber wolf."

Muriel decided against making comments about endangered wildlife, knowing cold weather would come and the house could be drafty. "You can use it to keep warm at night."

Sharona then suddenly looked around the room, her eyes wide, as if hearing something that Muriel could not. "This place is a little haunted, right?"

"Huh? Oh, well," Muriel wasn't sure how to answer. She needed the money and hoped more people would come and stay to help out with the electric bill, the multitude of repairs, and other household expenses that needed to be paid. "Well, old houses are drafty sometimes, and the pipes get noisy. That's all."

"It's okay," Sharona said. "I think there's only one ghost, and I'm sure we'll get along just fine. I usually get along pretty good with ghosts and other people from the spirit world. I'm just so glad to be out of that motel."

Muriel wanted to ask if she was clairvoyant, but wondered if that could be considered a personal question of some sort. "Well, let me show you the room."

Sharona picked up her things and followed Muriel up the stairs.

"There's a bathroom right across the hallway from your room, and the light in there is a little dim, but I'll fix it when I can."

Laura came to Rick's house with Zelda and they nearly talked all night long. It was too late then for Rick to take Rufus out to meet anyone and so they decided to wait until the next night after Rick closed up the art gallery on the lower floor of the house where he sold his work. At that time a few other local businesses might still be open, also, and Rufus could start learning his way around. They walked through the downtown business district where the tourists wandered after spending their day on the beach, as people tended to either shop or visit clubs after hours.

"So I guess your girlfriend isn't rich anymore, huh?"

"She grew up with every material thing you could imagine, but was never loved. What would you rather have, Rufus?"

"I never felt loved, either. My mother ignored me, then one of my stepfathers started beating me up."

"Your mother didn't intervene?"

"Naw. I guess she was just sick of me being around, anyway. She needed him to pay the bills, so she told me if I didn't like it, then to get the hell out."

"So you ended up on the street?"

"That's where most kids end up, Rick. Or I guess that's where kids like me go, anyway. I tried staying in a shelter. It didn't work out."

"How come the shelter didn't work out?"

"One of the guys who worked there was a creep. Anyway, I ended up on the street and ended up doing bad stuff to survive anyway. Maybe I should have stayed in the shelter. There was only one creep at the shelter. There's a lot more like that on the streets at night. Especially in this town. They say any place where people go for vacation, there's a lot of stuff going on."

"Yeah? How come nobody seems to know this?"

"What? About kids being on the street? Or kids selling themselves? I don't know. Maybe because no one cares. It's like how there's so much drugs on the street, and so many people doing drugs. They don't just sell themselves for food, you know. Some people get into drugs, and they'll do anything for drugs. It's all around. But no one seems to notice, unless you're right there in it. I mean, the people who live in the nice houses, who eat in those nice restaurants all over town, the people who lay on the beach and shop in the nice stores, they don't know it because they don't see it. It's like there's a whole world that people don't know about. People living in cars and stuff."

Rick listened and sighed, "Well, I don't know what to tell you. Come on." Rick headed toward one of the shops, "Let's go in this one. You might find it interesting."

They walked into *Antique Emporium*. The first thing Rufus noticed was the framed poster that hung on the wall opposite the entranceway; it said, "Overthrow the People!" On the desk where the cash register was, there brightly glowed a lava lamp. Next he noticed vast amounts of vinyl records. He had seen records before; a few gathering dust in the basement of his mother's house, ignored and forgotten, but he had not seen so many together in one place. He quickly flipped through them, not recognizing any of the names on them: Rush, Dylan, the Doobie Brothers, Three Dog Night, the Beatles, Simon and Garfunkel, Paul Revere and the Raiders, Peter, Paul, and Mary, John Denver, the Grass Roots, the Moody Blues, the Byrds,

Hendrix, Pete Seeger, the Who, and many others he had never heard of before.

"People still listen to this stuff?"

"Rufus, this is real music." Rick emphasized the word *real.* "It's much better than the garbage people hear today."

The lady behind the counter tried to stifle a laugh, but could not.

On the shelf above the bin of vinyl records there was a yellow plastic toy. Rufus stared at it and could not quite figure out what it was supposed to be.

"It's a yellow submarine," the lady called over from where she stood. "You know. A yellow submarine."

"He's too young to remember," Rick turned and said to her. "He won't get it. I'll explain it to him later. Hey, Rufus, check out all these old books, here." Rick gestured toward a tall wooden bookcase that stood next to the bin where the records were kept and pulled a book out. "Get a load of this one."

Rufus stared at it. "What? It says, *Steal This Book?* Who would name a book like that?"

"I had several copies," the lady said. "But they kept disappearing. If you want that, it's ten dollars."

Rick returned it and pulled out a few others. "Some of these are considered classics, you know, Rufus. *On the Road.* Here's another that was popular a while ago, *The Prophet.* Oh, and this was made into a movie." It was *The Stepford Wives.* He put it back. "Here's one that kids used to like, although it was more popular with girls." He pulled out *The Message in the Hollow Oak,* by Carolyn Keene. "Never mind." He put it back. "Come meet my friend Justina."

She leaned on the desk and smiled. "You must be Rufus. Rick told me about you. It's nice to meet you."

"Hi," he said simply, with his hands in the pockets of his baggy jeans. He noticed that she looked to be quite young, but probably was not. She wore a long, gray velvet and lace top and

35

slightly faded black jeans, her brown hair pulled up into a bun atop her head with a few stray curls hanging down around her face. He also realized she was pretty, and knew she could be way too old for him. "Hi," he repeated.

"Want me to show you the rest of the store?" she asked. "I was going to close soon, but you're here, so I'll show you around."

She walked into the back area beyond where the sixties items were kept and he followed along, not quite knowing what he should be looking at. On a peg on the wall hung a long mink stole made of several complete mink pelts with paws, tails, and heads with glass eyes. Justina pulled it off the peg and wrapped it around her shoulders. "Isn't this a riot? I love these. I had a lot like this in stock, but this is one of my last ones. I might not sell this one. I might just keep it. It's old, but it's in good shape."

He looked around and saw antique machinery lined up on shelves and countertops, as if waiting to be taken by someone that would make them useful again. There were manual typewriters, old radios, and items Rufus could not even identify.

"What's that thing?" he asked, pointing at it and not comprehending what it was. It was made of metal, painted black, and appeared to have a microphone or speaker of some kind, with wires attached.

"It's a telephone," she said.

"Huh? That's a phone?"

"That's what we call a candlestick phone. They were popular in the nineteen thirties. I think they're much more elegant than the contraptions people have today. But you couldn't carry that around with you."

"And what's that thing?" He pointed at another machine he didn't recognize. It had a wooden base, a hand crank, with what appeared to be a large horn sticking up out of it.

"It's an old type of record player. It's called a Victrola. You crank it and put a record on it, and it plays. It doesn't need electricity."

"Cool."

"Someday," she said, "the things we use today will be considered antiques. Come back in fifty years and see what ends up in here."

He looked around. There were glass cases filled with antique toys, fragile porcelain dolls, and more cases filled with antique jewelry, some of which looked to be valuable.

"I'll have to remove those and put them in the safe before closing up," she said, and she put the mink stole back where it was.

"Well, come on Rufus," Rick called after him from the front of the store. "She needs to close up soon."

"Okay. Thanks for showing me your store."

"Hey kid," she said. "You seem kind of down."

"He's still getting used to the idea," Rick said, leaning against the bookcase and going through a copy of *Serpico* by Peter Maas. "I know someone who should read this." But he put it back. "He didn't know his real father, you see."

"Oh," she understood. "Well, Rufus, it's not that bad, really. Just don't believe any of that nonsense you see on TV, okay?"

"Thanks," he said again, and finally smiled, if only slightly.

He walked out following Rick back into the night.

"Now if you run a business like that," Rick said, "it's a good idea to have someone work for you during the day. I used to have someone to mind the gallery, but found out he was taking cash from the cash register. So," he sighed, "I don't have anyone right now." He continued on, "Let's go into that one, a few doors down."

In the dark of night the house was quiet and with no sign of any life except the sounds of the few mice that skittered about.

37

The she-wolf padded silently down the stairs, sensing another type of presence. She drifted into the small room that was used as a library, and saw the man seated and writing at a small dark wooden desk. He dressed in an out of date sort of manner, as if he had just stepped out of history, or out of an old film. He put down his fountain pen and turned to look at her.

Well, you're an unusual sort of creature, aren't you?

She stared back at him, silent and motionless.

Everyone now just refers to me as the Professor, everyone who is still living, that is. I do hear them mention me in conversation, from time to time, so I suppose they remember me. I did not die here, but I lived here. And here I remain. I do think she knows I'm here. But she pretends that she doesn't notice me. I don't know why. But what does it matter? I really don't know why I stay here, when I could go on to a better place. Perhaps one day I shall. It could be that I stay because people I care about are still here. I see them every once in a while, drifting in and drifting out of this old place. Sometimes I see my beloved, also. The one who still remains here on this Earth, long after the fatal encounter I had. Dear God, I wish I could hold her in my arms again.

I thought that creatures like you were only legend, but there you are. That's why you can see me, I suppose. I did discover that vampires also were a local reality, quite a while ago, before my sad departure into this realm. No, don't worry. It was just a foolish mortal man who killed me. Shot me dead.

And what brings you to our humble home? Can't talk in that form, can you? Well, I suppose not.

The wolf came closer and sat next to his chair, staring up at him.

But apparently you understand me. I did research folklore when I taught at the University, and made some amazing discoveries during my own research. Of course, if I had a chance to continue with my research, perhaps I could have looked more deeply into the theory that legends of shapeshifters are a distant memory of shamanistic practices that were common so long ago before civilization took hold, of the adepts who walked into the spirit world taking the form of a wolf, or some other creature. And there you are. And I suppose you and I both know you can learn so much while travelling on this side. There, I just learned something new, that werewolves still stalk the night. It proves you don't ever have to stop learning, even after you're dead.

I suppose you must see some amazing things in your wanderings, don't you? If only you could tell me. Come by and visit in your human form, if you can. You can tell me all about it.

I thought I might see the one who did me in, drifting in though the ether. When I woke up on this side, after a while I heard people say he was sent to the gallows, and thought I'd see him. I half expected his revenant to come to apologize for his idiocy. But no. It took me a while and finally I realized that he probably went straight to Hell. Of course there must be such a place. There is the higher realm, which I haven't gotten around to visiting; then there are the lower levels of existence, the lowest level of which some of course call Hell, and there is this in-between place, where the living cannot often see us or hear us, but we are indeed here. And then of course there is the world the living call the real world, the material world. But after spending time here, I wonder which is the real world after all.

He looked directly into her dark wolfish eyes.

I don't have many other creatures to talk to. Not here. Spirits do pass through on occasion. Out there in the forest, there is the ghost of an old Indian. I see him, but not very often. Oh well. Really. I don't know why I stay in this place.

He turned away and went back to his work, then looked up again.

I seem to be writing the same notes over and over and over, as if repeating all the things I did while I was living. Oh well, I suppose that's what ghosts do. It's quite dull, really. And there's no sense of time here. I don't seem to know how long I've been dead. Decades perhaps, but I don't know for sure.

I imagine you must have your own wolfish business to attend to. I won't keep you. Do come back and visit again. It was awfully nice to meet you.

She stood up and drifted out, then down the hallway, and out through the back door, into the dark of night to explore the forests and fields behind the old house.

Muriel's car came off the highway and onto the long and lonely dark country road that led into the small town, struggling to keep awake after another late night class at college. She meant to ask someone in the office why the course was only offered at night, but she never got around to it. If she wanted to graduate this year, she needed to take this class and finish it, even if she did fall asleep halfway through the deadly boring lecture.

She rounded a corner, then turned onto the street that led up to her house. She was finally truly beginning to think of it as her home instead of an old building she had been burdened with. Her car drifted slowly up the quiet lane, about to turn into the driveway.

Suddenly she hit the brakes.

"Oh my God!" She swerved to avoid hitting an animal as it ran across the road.

It was a wolf.

"Oh my God," she said again. She had seen wolves in a zoo once, but had never seen one running free. She wondered if she should report it, or if it even mattered in a town surrounded by so much forest. She imagined there could be bears and wolves and all sorts of wildlife in the woods around town. She had been in the rural area for almost a year, and so far had seen wild turkeys, coyotes, deer, raccoons, woodchucks, and an assortment of other wildlife she never expected to see in her backyard.

Her car finally pulled into the driveway. She opened the car window to look around the driveway before getting out. She had heard once before that wolves, despite their fierce reputation, rarely attacked people, and she hoped that were true.

She warily got out of the car and hurried inside.

Once inside she flipped on a light switch and removed her jacket and put it in the closet, then climbed heavily up the stairs toward her room so she could finally collapse onto her bed and sleep.

Halfway up the stairs she saw the door to Sharona's room suddenly open. There she stood, in her pink pajamas, the wolf pelt she brought with her wrapped around her shoulders like a shawl.

"Oh, I didn't mean to wake you," Muriel said.

Sharona yawned. "No, you didn't wake me. Maybe I was just having a dream. Goodnight." And she closed the door.

Muriel continued walking down the semi-darkened hallway and into her own room at the end of the hall. And then she realized the strange coincidence. She had never seen any wolves around before now. Could it be possible? Other strange things were possible. She had learned that while living in the small town.

They continued to walk the pavement under the streetlights while passing by vacationers, some alone, and some with their families. Rufus wondered if he had gone through every vampire-owned business or trinket shop in town. He also learned that it was good to have a jewelry store next to a bar, because people are more likely to make unnecessary purchases after having a few drinks. There was also a pawnshop advertising, "We Buy and Sell Gold" with items stocking the shelves that were probably more unusual and eclectic than the antique store. And further down the street away from the shops there was a mechanic who worked very late into the night, and who asked Rick how the old car was running. They had been wandering several hours and then suddenly he noticed Rick turning to go down into a dark alleyway. "Come on, Rufus."

But Rufus stopped and looked warily into the darkness. "What's down there?"

"Another establishment, sort of; but it's private. Most people don't come down here. Most people aren't allowed down here. Also, it's the only place in town you can get drinks for free." Rick continued on down into the alley, and Rufus followed, mostly because he did not know his way back.

"Is that the place you say you guys all hang out?"

"Yes," Rick said. "You don't have to go, if you don't want to, but I'm going."

"Well, I don't know the way back, I don't think."

"It's easy," Rick said. "Just go up that way about two blocks," he pointed, "then take that left before the gas station—"

"I don't have the key to the house," Rufus said, still hanging back near the entrance to the alley.

"Oh." Rick reached into the pocket of his leather jacket. "Okay."

"Naw." Rufus suddenly changed his mind. "Maybe I'll go with yah."

"Well, come on."

He followed Rick past trashcans and large stacked up cardboard boxes and crates. "We used to have a small dim light over the door, but too many people wandered down into the alley, not the kind of people we want to come this way, either. The boxes are stacked up to block the view, so no one sees the door." And then he descended down some steps into an entrance that led into the basement of the brick building that faced the street. "I would say this is sort of like a speakeasy, but I don't think you would know what I was talking about. No one is supposed to know this place exists, you got that, Rufus?" He reached for the set of keys from out of his pocket again. "We used to leave the door unlocked, but we had to change that, too."

Rufus saw over the door a small glass panel with a small amount of light glowing through it; in ornate lettering etched into the glass it said, "After Dark."

"That's what we like to call it," Rick said.

They walked in and Rufus noticed how comfortably dim the lighting was, without glare and just enough light to see well. Classical music played, the volume turned down low, just enough to be heard. The walls were covered in dark wood paneling, where a few paintings and a small tapestry hung. People sat clustered around small tables, or sat at the bar, some talking, and some simply sat quietly.

Rick saw one man sitting at a table alone, and so he drifted over and pulled out a chair. Rufus followed, not wanting to be separated. He then froze, looked around, and realized he was surrounded by vampires, until suddenly he remembered that he was one himself.

"Here, take a seat, Rufus," Rick said.

"So you're the kid," the man said as Rufus sat. He held an ornate cut crystal glass half filled with blood.

"Yeah," Rufus said, not knowing what else to say.

"Rick is my brother," the man said. "So remember that I am the only one who is allowed to make him feel miserable."

"Okay," Rick said. "Alex, this is Rufus. Rufus, this is Alex. He is very much older than me, so that's why he's such a grouch. Now who picked out the soundtrack for this evening? It must have been you, Alex. Shut that thing off and put some real music on."

"Want me run back down the street and get some old records?" Rufus asked.

"He's finally getting a sense of humor, this kid," Rick said. "I'm bringing him around tonight to meet people. We can't find his father so I might as well take him in."

A waitress came by with a tray and three more glasses were deposited on the table, one in front of each of them.

Rufus stared at it, then finally reached for it. "Whatever."

A few nights later Muriel and Josephine came to visit Annasophia's small but comfortable home. Besides her connection with Muriel's granduncle, she was the oldest vampire in the area, and seemed to know more about the past than anyone. Finally Muriel decided to get up the courage to ask, although she still felt foolish to even think such a thing. But when she talked to Josie on the phone, Josie told her that Sergeant Stepanek had seen a wolf, also. In fact, he had seen the wolf nearby Sharona's car when she first arrived in town.

Josie gave a rundown of what she knew of Sharona after they arrived at Sophie's house, that she had lived with her grandparents, and their house burned down. She ended up in a foster home, but quickly left when she realized the foster father was "bothering" the young girls in the home. Sharona then hit the road, driving as far away as she could, not wanting to be found and put back into another foster home, sleeping in her car, and then finally ending up working as a waitress and renting a room in Muriel's old house.

"She sure sounds like she's had a tough time," Muriel said. She sat on the soft broken-in old couch next to Sophie's gray tabby cat and took a sip from the cup of herbal tea that Sophie had offered her.

"Well, she seems like a nice kid," Josie said. "And she's a hard worker." Josie stood in front of a dress form aiming her digital camera to take a picture of a gown Sophie had completed. It was created of mauve satin with embroidered black roses climbing up the long skirt. The photograph would be put on the website that Josie had helped to set up for Sophie to sell her work as a dressmaker: handmade wedding gowns, ball gowns, prom dresses, and any high fashion request made to order. But Annasophia had no computer. When orders came in, Josie printed them out and brought them to her.

"Isn't that beautiful?" Sophie asked. "Just like something a movie star would wear. And a lot of work went into it," she paused, and then looked directly at Muriel. "Now, Josie has already told me that you have an odd sort of question."

"Sophie," Muriel said, "I feel kind of stupid to even ask a question like this."

"That's alright, dear. Who else is there to ask?"

"Well," Muriel sighed, "I don't know."

Sophie continued on, "Stories of werewolves come from two different sources, Muriel. Some people have a condition in which they grow a vast amount of fur all over themselves. People like that were forced to work in freak shows, and that was the only thing that they could do for work, to survive. These poor people look like something from a bad horror film, and most horror films are bad."

It didn't take long for Muriel to learn that vampires did not enjoy horror films, mostly because of the negative way they were always portrayed. Muriel gazed at Annasophia while she continued speaking; the fashionable gowns contrasted with the plain clothes their creator wore: long brown corduroy skirt and an old soft sweater, with her dark blonde curls kept in order with simple tortoiseshell side combs. No one would ever imagine she was a wise old vampiress with well over two hundred years' experience surviving hardship of many kinds. To most people, she appeared to be a simple seamstress from an almost unknown little town. She looked to be about forty but carried herself with the kind of dignity and grace that only a

45

long life could give. She spoke while the girls listened closely, "And then there are the types of werewolves from whence the legends actually came from in the first place, many thousands of years ago, before history was written. I have only a few centuries of memories, Muriel, dear, but I was told these stories when I myself was very young, in the old country, by those much older than me."

"So, Sophie, is this really possible?" Muriel asked, finally looking away from the beautiful dress and looking directly at Annasophia.

"Muriel, it is not possible for anyone to change into an animal. That would defy all natural law. However, the change would not be physical." She finished removing the gown from the dress form and put it on a hanger to be stored away later. "Are you perhaps familiar with what some people today call astral projection?"

Muriel thought a moment, "That's when you go out of your body, right?"

"Right." Sophie went to mount another gown onto the dress form, this time of turquoise blue velvet. "That is a modern term for what people called just simply the spirit leaving the body, to travel into the spirit world, walk on the other side of things, and such. Long ago, before history was written down, so I have been told, all through Europe during the dark ages there were people living as if in tribes, the Celts and the Gauls and countless others; they lived the way primitive people lived, in the forest, living off the land, in simple huts. The people were mostly helpless against the forces of nature, and at the mercy of other warlike people. You see, Muriel," she said as she straightened the fabric so Josie could take another picture, "to understand where werewolves come from, you need to know a little of how things were, very long ago, before my time, before my mother's time, before her mother's time. We know things because these stories were passed down through the ages."

The camera flashed, and Sophie went to remove the gown and put another on the dress form for display. Muriel commented that the blue was the most beautiful she had seen so far.

"Thank you, it's another favorite of mine. Well, anyway. The people back then, they were mostly warriors, but there were also healers, hunters, shepherds, artisans, and sorcerers, or men and women they called sorcerers. Today maybe they would be called shamans, people whose spirit travelled to the other side to gain knowledge, or rid the village of evil spirits. There were always those who were born with a gift of sight, and there were always those who learned to use this gift. They trained starting very young to develop their powers of the mind, which then people believed to be magic. One thing that some shamans learned to do was to have their spirit take the form of an animal when they walked over to the other side. In that way, they were considered to be shapeshifters. Sometimes they took the form of a bear, but the wolf was the most common, I believe. The primitive people always held the wolf in high esteem; not like today. People think they are just useless vermin. People learned to hunt by watching wolves hunt. The first dogs were wolves. Wolves were a gift when man still lived in dark caves; they protected the people from enemies and helped the hunters bring back game. Thousands of years ago, the wolf was considered strong and wise. So when the shapeshifter went into the spirit world, he would go as a wolf. He, or she, would wear a fur that still held some essence of the beast, even though the wolf's own spirit had long passed on. So these sorcerers became shapeshifters, they would put the part of the pelt where the head of the wolf would be over their own head, go into a dreamlike state, and as their soul left their body a spectral wolf would walk the land, a wolf able to see the other side, and go do whatever they had to do to help their people. Maybe the wolf would scare off bandits, or drive off troublesome spirits.

47

Whatever that needed to be done, the shaman who was a shapeshifter would become a spectral wolf to go and do it. And they used to say in the old days, the most powerful of these sorcerers could send their spirits all the way to the moon and see into the night sky and look out into the beyond at the other worlds. But I do not know if that is true, having never known anyone who actually could do such things myself."

Muriel was almost kept silent as her sense of wonder and amazement awakened inside of her, but she finally asked, "But, Sophie, why would they become like an animal to do that? Why couldn't they just be themselves, if they were going into the spirit world?" She stressed the word if, still not certain if she believed it.

"The spirit world is populated by creatures you cannot see, Muriel. And no, I can't see them, either, though I wish I could. But from what I have learned in the past, I know there does exist a world parallel to this one we exist in, another realm, populated by the otherworldly. The ancients knew of this. Sometimes people see ghosts, but usually you just hear ghosts, or feel a presence. But there are many things in the spirit world that can only be seen when you are over there. There are good things, and there are bad things, in the spirit world. You may meet spirits that are good, and maybe most of them are. Most creatures of the otherworld are harmless, Muriel. But if you meet something evil, it's better to be in some form that can be as fierce as they are."

"I didn't know any of this, Sophie," Josie said, taking a third picture, this time of a sky blue satin dress with lace trim. "How come you never told me any of this?"

"Well, you are so busy with work and school and life in general. I would have told you when you were older, perhaps. And I wasn't sure if you would be interested. Young people today are more interested in their machines, which have their uses, of course." She removed the satin dress and put it away with the others. "Spirits are all around us, girls, we usually just don't see them or hear them. Sometimes they can't appear, even if they want to. It's like there is a veil between the worlds," she sighed. "Loved ones pass on and sometimes their spirits linger, but we don't usually see them, even if they are there. It may be possible that they do see us, however.

"I do have one sad memory of a werewolf, long ago," she continued, finally sitting down. "When I was very young, and it was a time when most people could not read or write, I was travelling and staying at an inn at a small village. I heard a commotion and looked outside from where I was staying. They were dragging a poor soul through the streets, accusing him of being a werewolf. They dragged him along in chains. He protested that he had done nothing wrong. A man walking behind the crowd carried a wolf skin, as proof I suppose. I looked away. The sight of it made me frightened. I worried they would find out what I was, and I would share his fate."

"What happened to him?" Josie asked, finally putting the camera in her purse and sitting down next to Muriel.

"They hanged him," she said flatly. "So, you see, they were still hunting werewolves in the nineteenth century. Muriel, I don't know if any people still follow these old ways today. People like us were hunted down mercilessly, and so were these people, shapeshifters, or werewolves if you want to call them that. It's something that goes back thousands of years. I cannot say if this girl is a werewolf or not. There may be people who still do this, but I do not know. Maybe it's all just coincidence. If she seems like a nice girl, then probably she's just a nice girl. A nice girl who is going through a hard time and sleeps with a warm fur for whatever small comfort it gives."

"I thought they would use silver bullets to kill werewolves?" Josie asked.

"This happened before all these ridiculous movies, dear," Sophie explained. "They would kill these people in all sorts of ways, hang them, burn them, and yes, shoot them, whether with silver or not."

"Sophie, I really appreciate your telling me," Muriel said, "I took folklore in college, and none of this is in books."

"Of course not," Sophie said. "We're not in your college books, either. We're not supposed to exist. But here we are."

"And there's another thing." Muriel finally finished her tea, and by now it had gone cold. "I think I have a ghost in my house."

"Well, that's news. Have you seen anything?" Sophie said, reaching to caress the sleeping cat.

"No, I just hear footsteps, and stuff. Sometimes the lights flicker, but maybe the wiring is bad. I don't know. I guess there's a lot more to this world than what we read in textbooks, and more than just what we can see with our eyes."

"Well, it's an old house, so many people there lived and died over time." She hesitated, and then changed the subject, "Now, there is something else I want to tell you girls." She reached into the pocket of the long brown cardigan she wore, and pulled out a neatly folded letter. "And soon I will have to show this to everyone, of course. Everyone, that is, Muriel, I mean others of our kind, as you already know about this; because you passed this on to me, but Josephine does not know about it. And I already went ahead and wrote back to them. You see, dear Muriel," she looked directly at her, "because of you, a miracle has happened." She then handed the letter to Josie. "Josephine, read it. We are not the last of our kind, after all."

Rick leaned against the counter in his art gallery while looking through the local newspaper and heard the door open. He looked up, expecting a customer.

"Laura, hey," he said, almost surprised.

"I've missed you," she said simply.

"Well, I've been around." He put the paper under the counter.

"But we haven't really seen each other that much, you know, I mean, we haven't been alone, since," she paused, "since you've taken on so much responsibility."

"He's a good kid. Drives me nuts sometimes, but he's a good kid. He just needs someone to set him straight, that's all."

"How is he?" She knew Rick had taken the boy in and encouraged him to get his high school equivalency diploma, while the other two boys from the street unfortunately landed back into trouble.

"Well, he's doing a little better now that he's met a few more of us and doesn't think we're all a pack of Bela Lugosi clones, plus he's no longer on the street." He came around and pulled her close. "I missed you, too."

"Yeah," she whispered.

"How's your grandmother? Zelda?"

"She's gone back to work at the mansion. She said she'd keep an eye on things there for me. It helps that he—the man I thought was my father—he still believes she doesn't understand much English. She thinks Mr. Rivers is up to no good, Rick." She leaned on him and he put his arms around her more tightly. "She says he's been talking on the phone to this man who," she paused and exhaled, "I think he's had people killed before. She says he's been talking to someone she thinks may even be," she hesitated again, "a hit man. She said I should be careful."

"But why would he do anything to you?" he asked, "You're out of his life now."

"He never liked to leave loose ends, I guess. I was a mistake. I was a reminder that my mother stopped loving him. Now I know why he was so awful to me."

"Try not to worry about it." But he knew that she would.

"He tried to kill me before, once; I didn't tell you, maybe because I wanted so badly to forget."

51

"Tried to kill you? How?"

"He owned a lot of horses, and when I was little, I took riding lessons. He told the stable manager which horse to put me on. But the stable manager would never let me ride the horse that Mr. Rivers said I should ride. The stable manager made sure I was on a quiet, gentle old horse. When my father— when Mr. Rivers found out, he demanded to know why. The stable manager said, 'That horse you want your daughter to ride is too mean for a little girl, she could get hurt.' So, he fired him. I realize now, that man probably saved my life, and lost his job for it."

He continued to hold her and silently listen.

"I don't even know who I really am now, but I'm glad I'm not the daughter of the powerful and feared billionaire Augustus James Rivers the Third. The things I've been reading about him lately, I'm lucky to have gotten away when I did. It's alleged he's behind all these terrible things, but no one dares touch him. He owned a factory that blew up several years ago; I knew that. But I'll tell you what I didn't know, until I left home. The workers wanted to unionize, and right around that time, there was this devastating accident. Only some people think it wasn't really an accident. A lot of people were killed, more than two hundred factory workers. They still don't know the exact cause of the explosion. Or maybe people who know are afraid to say."

"I've heard that too, from the reporter I told you about. He knows all the bad news and conspiracy theories. So, what is your real name, then?" He looked down at her sad face and smiled.

"Laura Blasko. I'm just plain Laura Blasko. My real father was a poor immigrant from Eastern Europe who worked as a gardener. I'm not even sure if he was in the country legally or not, and I don't care."

His hand reached to brush her fawn colored hair away from her neck. "It has been a long time . . ."

Just then two people walked into the gallery.

"Oh look at all the pretty pictures, honey, we just gotta get one for living room." The woman wore a large pink nylon fanny pack so her hands could be free to carry her multiple shopping bags.

"Phyllis." An overweight and balding red faced man followed her in. "You just keep on running up my credit cards on all these stupid souvenirs you buy."

Rick released Laura and stood up straight; he looked over toward the two people who had just wandered in and they seemed to not notice anything but the artwork. "I'll tell you what, Laura, why don't you go up and check on Rufus and make sure he's studying?"

"Okay," she sighed and then slowly ascended the stairs to the second floor where Rick lived, and where Rufus had also found shelter from the dark streets.

Rufus sat at Rick's small wooden kitchen table surrounded by a few books and crumpled up balls of paper all scattered about.

"How are you, Rufus?"

"Huh?" He looked up. "Oh, Miss Rivers. Hi. What's up?"

"Well, I guess Rivers isn't my real name anymore. But it's on my driver's license and all my other documents. I guess I'm going to have to figure out what to do about all that."

"Wow. Yeah." He had overheard most of the conversation when Laura had brought her grandmother to visit Rick.

"So, how's school?"

"It's dull, but Rick says I gotta do it so I won't grow up to be dumb. He's gonna make me grow up to be a decent vampire whether I like it or not and he keeps reminding me that a hundred years from now I'll probably thank him, and I can't like a girl until I'm thirty, but I guess it's better than living in a broken down old truck. And, oh, yeah, I still don't know what happened to my real father. The private eye dude can't find him."

She pulled out a chair and sat down next to him. "I'm sorry about that Rufus. But you know, Rick is right. You need to finish school, and you just need to keep your life straight. There's a lot of trouble out there, and he doesn't want anything to happen to you."

"I know. He says none of us can just do whatever we want, even vampires have to follow rules."

"That's right, Rufus. Only a few people in this world can do whatever they want to do; men like Mr. Rivers, men who have enough money to buy power. And you know what? In a few decades, he'll be dead. What good will all his money do for him then? You'll be alive many years from now, and maybe someone will mention an oil spill that happened a century ago, an oil spill that never got properly cleaned up, and you'll say, 'I think that oil company belonged to a man named Augustus Rivers,' and people will say, 'Who was he?'"

"Yeah, but right now, I'm real bored. I miss Jimmy and Charlie, even though they're idiots. And I wish someone could find my dad. And I just don't understand any of this stuff."

She thought that maybe Rufus could not understand how his life had suddenly changed so drastically, realizing that his father was a vampire, and that he would inherit those traits, and all the adjustments he would need to make now. She was sympathetic. "What don't you understand?"

"This stupid algebra."

"Oh." She took the book. "Well, let's see if we can work on it together, Rufus. Maybe we can figure out this stupid algebra."

Josie drove Muriel home and pulled up into her driveway. "Well, that was interesting. So you've got a ghost and a werewolf in your house. I never knew about any of that stuff that happened long ago. I wish Sophie had told me these things before, so I wouldn't be surprised by it now."

"I didn't know any of that stuff either. Like I said, that's not exactly stuff they teach in college," said Muriel. "Well, hey, if vampires exist, then why not ghosts and werewolves."

"But real werewolves aren't at all like what you see on TV, and neither are vampires," Josie said, putting the car in park so Muriel could get out.

"I know. Nothing on TV is real. I guess I should just sit in my front yard and watch all the paranormal creatures walk by. And I thought this little town would be dull when I first moved here." She opened the car door. "Hey, thanks for bringing me over to talk to Sophie. I really thought she'd think I was nuts."

"That's okay." She noticed there was a light on in Muriel's house. "She must be back from work. I'll go in and say hi to her."

"Okay. But I don't think we should say anything to her, about, well, you know."

"Yup," Josie quickly agreed. "We could be wrong. And if we're not wrong, maybe she doesn't want to tell us, for whatever reason."

When they got in they found Sharona in her pajamas sitting at the kitchen table with a cup of tea and with an anguished look on her face. "Oh hi, Muriel. Hi Josie."

"Sharona, you look upset," Josie asked. "What's wrong?"

"Oh, you know the guy who bothers the waitresses? I waited on his table tonight. He pulled a roll of bills out of his pocket and asked me to meet him out where his truck was parked."

"Oh, that is so gross," Muriel said. "Did you tell the manager?"

"No. I don't want to lose my job."

"He does that to all of us," said Josie. "One night a girl actually went out to his truck, and they fired her for it. But no one says anything to him. He's a regular customer, so we have to put up with him."

"Well, that stinks," Sharona said, finishing her tea. "But I'd better keep my job, no matter what. Oh well. I'm going to bed. They asked me to do another shift tomorrow." She stood up and washed the teacup in the sink, dried it and put it away. "I guess I won't take it personal, if he does that to everybody. See yah at work, Josie. Thanks again for warning me about that creep. Good night."

Muriel watched Sharona go up the stairs toward her room. "That's awful. Why don't they ban him from the place?"

"He's a good customer," Josie sighed. "So we can't do anything about him. Besides, I think he's friends with the owner."

"Well, it's just not right."

The décor of Laura's apartment was a great contrast to the upper floor of the old house where Rick resided. The furnishings were all new, with couch and matching chairs of genuine black leather. The carpets were also new, and the high-end kitchen appliances appeared barely used. And the large windows, facing east, would prevent him from staying much longer.

Her bedroom was equally luxurious, but less well organized than the living room, with items of clothes, shoes, scarves, fashion magazines, jewelry and makeup all scattered about. In an expensive cut crystal vase, next to the small television on her bureau, were several tall peacock feathers, lending a slight bohemian touch.

She was next to him, half asleep; he pulled her closer and then reached to caress the small wound on her throat. She stirred and sighed, "I wish you would stay longer."

"I can't. You know that."

"I know. I just wish you would stay longer, and—"

"Then you'd get anemic. So I can't do that, either. Not that I wouldn't like to. Thank you for helping Rufus with his school work."

"He's a nice kid." She opened her eyes and watched him get up and prepare to leave. "He said he loved the antique store you took him to."

"He did? I thought he was bored." He sat at the edge of the bed pulling his short black leather boots on. "He seemed so bored in that store, I'm surprised he even noticed he was there."

"He said he's been visiting Jimmy in the drug rehab. Did you know that?" She sat up and watched as he went to gaze out the window and look up at the sky.

"No, I didn't know that." He turned to look at her. "I guess the kid doesn't tell me everything."

"He's been taking the bus to go visit him late in the afternoon, before you get up. Maybe he thinks you wouldn't want him to still hang around with him." She got up to stand beside him and watch the sky. She leaned against him and he wrapped both arms around her.

"I don't care who that boy hangs around with, as long as he stays off the street, and keeps out of trouble." He bent to kiss her throat, having one last small taste before he had to leave. He noticed a small red drop stained her white satin and lace nightgown, and that she seemed not to care.

"He says Jimmy practically interrogates him about all sorts of things now."

"Really? Why? What does he say?"

"Oh, I don't know. He says Jimmy asks him all kinds of ridiculous questions, about whether or not he's a real vampire yet, is he drinking blood yet, does he think he's better than us normal people now, those kinds of questions."

Rick laughed quietly. "I suppose Rufus could just say, 'Yes, yes, and no.' Jimmy had better be careful, he could end up in a psych ward if people overhear him. I won't tell Rufus you told

57

me. He'll probably tell me himself when he gets around to it. Charlie is the one I worry about. He's the one who's in jail. He's a skinny little kid. Someone in that hell hole is going to . . . never mind."

"I know," she sighed. "It's a tough world. It didn't take me long to learn that. But I never stop being shocked by some of the things that go on."

They watched as the dark sky slowly began to brighten; in the distance, the stars began to fade and disappear. Far off, they could see the sun just beginning to touch the sky. It was beyond the time for him to leave.

"I used to drive out to the desert and park the old car and lay on top of the hood and stare up at the stars, just look into the sky and wonder what's out there, or just look up and think about nothing. Did you ever do that? Drive out to where there's no people, and just look up at the night sky?"

"No," she said simply, "but if you go out there again, take me with you."

"I will." he released her. "I wish I could stay."

"I know."

He left. She heard him walk out and close the door behind him. She sighed. She looked out the window and down into the parking lot to see him go out to his car. It was easy for her to find his car in the parking lot; it was the only red 1968 convertible in a lot filled with new Toyotas, Hondas, Saabs, and a few BMW's. The old car slowly drifted out of the parking lot and onto the street.

Then she noticed someone else. It was odd to see a man wandering through the parking lot this early, before dawn. And he was hovering near her BMW, as if looking at the rear license plate. Why? She shivered inside. She wished she could imagine he was just admiring a nice car.

But she knew better than to think it was as harmless as that.

Josephine went to collect the payment left on the table and decided she didn't care if the man hadn't left her a tip. She guessed that maybe he didn't, because he was behaving like his usual self, 'C'mon, why don't yah smile, honey?' And she didn't. Instead, she simply said, 'Is there anything else I can get for you?' And then she realized her mistake for even asking. He looked up at her and said, 'I know what you can get for me, little cutie . . .' He began to describe in graphic and horrific detail, so she simply walked away quietly.

She returned to the table when he was finally gone and found that he had left no tip and that the payment was several dollars short; he had also written something disgusting to her on a napkin. She debated internally whether to keep it as evidence, but decided to throw it away. What good would it do to keep it?

She made eye contact with other waitresses who were clustered around the cash register, and they looked back at her. They were talking and laughing, but when they saw the look on her face they all stopped giggling and together their faces went cold, silently understanding what she was putting up with. "Oh, no, what did he say?" one of the girls asked as she passed by. But she didn't want to answer. Instead, she looked back and just said, "The usual."

She kept walking until she made it back to kitchen. Maybe she would go home and claim she was sick. She certainly felt sick inside after hearing just the beginning of what her least favorite customer had to say to her. She knew better than to tell the manager. 'Lighten up,' he would always say. 'He's just kidding around with you. You need to get a sense of humor about it. It's part of your job to deal with customers.'"

It was useless to complain.

There was not much she could do until she was finished with college and found a better job. But how many good jobs were there that could be done only at night? She sighed, inhaling and letting it out slowly. She hoped the lady who answered the telephones during the night shift at the town's small police station would hurry up and retire. She had already put an application in, and hoped, and waited.

She stood by the time clock and wondered whether to leave early. Suddenly she heard a commotion coming from the front of the restaurant near the entranceway. She recognized the voice. It was him. He had come back in and now he was yelling hysterically.

She went back out into the front area to see what he was worked up about, wondering if maybe some girl in the parking lot had kicked him or something.

"It was a wolf!" he screamed. "It went for my throat! There's a wolf out there! A wolf! I am telling you, there is a wolf!"

She walked back over where the other girls were standing. "Oh my God. What happened?"

They all stood and watched. The manager was talking to him and she heard him say, "Now, just calm down. It's probably just a stray dog."

"It was a wolf!" He turned and pointed at the door. "I didn't even make it to my truck! That thing went for me out there. I'm lucky to be alive! I could've been killed! I didn't have my gun with me. I left it at home!"

The girls stared and listened as he went on and on about the wolf, that it was huge, and it roared and pounced on him like a tiger, but he jumped out of the way; he thought it would chase him all the way back inside but it had disappeared out there somewhere in the dark. It could be anywhere out there. People had better look out, it was a killer.

"Hi guys." It was Sharona, suddenly appearing from behind the crowd. "Sorry I'm late. I . . . uh . . . had to stop and get some gas; my car was on empty."

"Oh, hi," Josie said, pretending not to notice any coincidence. "Did you see what happened?"

"N-no. But I wouldn't take anything he says too seriously."

"Yeah. You're right," Josie agreed. "He probably just tripped over one of those cute little Chihuahua dogs and landed on his fat red nose."

The girls all laughed.

"Back to work, girls." The manager saw them standing around and barked, "The party is over."

The girls all scattered to pick up dishes and wipe down tables with the hope of collecting a few decent tips. Sharona went to help some other girls clean up a table where a large group had been, and it was a mess. Josie looked over her shoulder and saw the manager walk out to the parking lot to have a look around. She knew he wouldn't find anything.

Shortly after the excitement died down police arrived; Sergeant Stepanek and another officer that Josie did not recognize. She remained in a distance, even though the Sergeant looked her way briefly before getting down to business.

"There is nothing out there," he said. "We were all through the area, there is no animal out there," he went on to reassure the manager. "It was probably just someone's dog that had gotten loose. That's all." He turned to the customer who was now sitting quietly alone in a booth by the entrance way and finishing a fourth beer that the manager said would be on the house. "Gary," the Sergeant addressed him by name since he had encounters with the man before, "why don't you go on home? Come on. We'll walk you to your truck."

Josie recalled that Sergeant Stepanek once mentioned that he had seen a wolf, and now wondered how much he knew, or what he suspected.

At the end of the shift, the waitresses all walked out together, and no one drove out of the parking lot until everyone's car started. Josie started her car, and let it run to warm the engine.

"Hey."

She looked out and saw Sharona's car pulled up beside hers, "What's up?"

"How did yah know?"

"Know what?" She pretended to be confused.

"Well, you know, how did you know it was me?"

Josephine hesitated a moment, and then said, "Okay, whatever, Sharona. Let me ask you this. How do you know that I know?"

"Josie, it was all over your face all night long. Especially when you made that crack about the little Chihuahua."

Josie laughed, "Okay. I give up. I guess I wouldn't win much at poker. Look, there's someone I want you to meet, and some things you should know about this little town. Do you want to stay up late and talk now, or do you want to talk about it later?"

Sharona hesitated, and gazed down at the dashboard of her Chevy. "Well, now is okay with me if it's okay with you."

"Fine. Why don't you get in my car and I'll tell you about it on the way."

"I am very pleased to meet you, Sharona." Annasophia sat down in a deep soft chair opposite Sharona and Josephine, who sat beside each other on the couch. "I hear you have talents that would impress even someone who has seen as much as I have."

"Well, ma'am," she began shyly, "my grandfather . . . he's the one who instructed me . . . he told me there were people like you . . . that people like you might still be around," she paused. "You're not what I expected."

Sophie smiled warmly. "You expected I would wear a long black gown?"

"N-no! No, ma'am. I didn't know what to expect. I thought maybe we'd drive up to a mansion, or something."

"We are just simple people, really, Sharona. Simple people who live by night. The horrible stories they tell about us are

62

untrue, as you probably may already know. And I know the horrible stories they tell of your kind are also quite untrue."

"Well, I'm pleased to meet you, too," she said. "I'm pretty much alone in this world, I guess." She stared sadly down at the floor. "My family is all dead now. I don't know anyone else like me. I might be the last, the last in the whole world."

"You don't know that, Sharona. In fact, we thought we were the last of our kind also, until recently. And I will tell you something; you are not the first of your kind that I have seen, although it was very long ago. I was not able to save him from the mob of people, but I want you to know that you are safe here. You will be safe in this town. You are no longer alone. You will have many friends here, for as long as secrets are kept and no trouble is started."

"I try to keep out of trouble, ma'am, I do try," she laughed quietly, wondering what Josie would say about that.

"I think she got rid of some trouble for us tonight, Sophie," Josie said. "I wish you had been there. She did a heck of a good job taking care of the pig that bothers all the girls who work at the truck stop."

"That guy totally overreacted. I mean, I barked at him and he freaked out. I couldn't have done anything to him, anyway. I'm not exactly solid when I'm like that, you know."

"I know, but it also may bring unwanted attention." Sophie looked at Sharona and smiled again. "None among us is perfect, either. I may have made a few mistakes of my own over the long years that have passed. But we won't talk about that. I'm glad you've found a place to stay with Muriel. She's a nice girl. She knows about us, and I'm sure she wouldn't mind knowing about you. In fact, she already suspects, since she saw a wolf run in front of her car. And please, call me Sophie."

"Thank you. I wondered if someday I would meet one of you, I mean . . . how can I say this? I was told people like you—vampires—were discovered in this town."

"By whom?" Sophie demanded quietly but firmly. "Not many people are supposed to know. We like to keep things quiet. Who told you, Sharona?"

"Well, there is a spirit in Muriel's house," she answered casually, as though having a spirit around one's home was quite normal and common. "You see, I often see ghosts or other beings when I go out as a wolf. He calls himself the Professor. He seems like a nice ghost, really. He just mentioned something about . . ."

Sophie froze, her eyes suddenly wide.

"I'm sorry. Did I say something wrong?"

"No, dear," Sophie answered quietly. "The ghost in Muriel's house is the Professor? But he didn't die there."

"N-no, but he stays there, to be close to people he cares about, I think."

"If I had only known he was there . . ."

"What would you do, Sophie?" Josie asked.

"I don't know," she said to Josie. "What could I do? Perhaps go over there and call out his name, tell him I have never forgotten him? I don't know." She looked at Sharona. "Thank you for letting me know. If you see him again, tell him for me, will you? That I have never forgotten him."

"I will, if I see him again, I'll try to tell him for you. I promise." She now recognized the pained and sad look in Annasophia's eyes; it was the same sadness that she carried deep within her own soul.

"It's not easy, Sharona, to lose someone you love."

"I know," she said, and a tear rolled slowly down her face. "I know . . ." And then Sharona broke down and began to sob uncontrollably.

Sophie got up and went to sit by her side. "That's right, I'm sure you do. And you're too young to have such sadness." She put her arm around her quivering shoulders. "Go ahead and cry. Cry for the both of us. My tears have almost all dried up over the centuries because of all the tragedy I have seen. Cry for all the ones we've all lost over the many years." She held her more tightly and continued to talk. "Before I came to this country, many of my people were killed. And so we came here. And when we came to this country, I lost even more of those that I loved. I hope to see them all again when I finally go to the beyond, but it won't be for a very long time. So if you see him, tell him that I will never love another."

Josie sat in silence, but reached to hold Sharona's hand.

"I'm sorry," Sharona sobbed. "I didn't mean to come here and cry like this. I'm so sorry . . ."

"It's okay," Josie said. "With all you've been through, I think you're holding up pretty well." She reached into her purse and got a handful of tissues.

"It's the first time I've really cried, since my grandparents were killed. I don't know why. Maybe because it was all so sudden, and because I've been just trying to keep my life together. They were killed by a drunken mob, calling my grandfather a werewolf." She struggled to regain her composure, and cleared her throat. "Which of course he was. . . . They were in the house, and the people set fire to the house. My grandfather made sure I got away."

"We know what it's like, Sharona," Annasophia said. "Some of us have faced things like this, also."

"I know death is not the end, because I see people who have passed over all the time, but I still miss them. I don't see them every day now. In fact, I saw them only once, since it happened. My grandfather used to tell me it's actually not easy for a ghost to appear to the living. They usually can just make noise most of the time." She took the tissues from Josie. "I really didn't mean to come here and fall apart like this."

Laura pushed the cart through the grocery store aisles and resisted the urge to look over her shoulder as she wandered through the dairy section, picking out various yogurts and reading labels to make sure they said "organic." She decided to try to convince herself that she was ridiculous to worry about the man who was apparently looking over her car as dawn came into the sky. She told herself that he was probably an early riser, just looking over her new BMW because it was a nice car. She tried to tell herself that, but in the back of her mind, she knew she should still worry.

She went to the frozen food section and remembered that Rick had gone into this grocery store with her one night when he had taken in the three street urchins; she recalled he made comments about the smell from the meat department and the lights being too bright. It was his first time in a grocery store, she realized. He had only gone in to get some things for the kids to eat.

She continued on and checked off items on her list, and picked out a few more that were not on her list; chocolate bars, which like many things, she was never allowed to have as a child, and a tabloid magazine on her way to the checkout line.

Out toward the parking lot she did catch herself looking around, as if watching for trouble, but she once again told herself she was being foolish. Why would Mr. Rivers even think about her now? She was out of his life. She tried to tell herself that. She was finally learning to enjoy living her own life, and she wasn't going to let him ruin it again.

She pulled the cart up beside her BMW and went to put the grocery bags on the rear seat, but dropped her keys. She bent to pick them up . . .

And heard the sound of glass shatter. Down around on the pavement where her keys were, she saw the sudden multiple shards of windshield glass from the white van that was parked behind her car. She knelt down and grabbed her keys, stayed under the rear of her car, and looked up. The van's windshield now had a large gaping hole in it. She then felt pieces of glass in her hair, and brushed them off so they would not get in her eyes. She did not know much about guns, but she knew enough to have heard that some guns have a "silencer;" and so that was probably why she only heard the sound of glass cracking and falling all over the pavement. She crawled under the rear bumper of her BMW and looked from her awkward position on the ground and watched the tires of another car speed away.

And she realized that if she had not dropped her keys on the pavement, it would have been all over.

"Oh . . . my . . . God."

She stood up, pieces of sharp glass falling off her. She quickly finished putting the items she bought into her car and drove out of the parking lot, fast. She got back to her apartment building and carried everything she bought together at once, so she would not need to go back out to her car.

Once inside her apartment, she locked the door behind her and picked up her phone. "Hello? Zelda? Grandma?" No answer. She left the message, "Oh my God, please call me back."

She slowly put the groceries into the refrigerator and wondered what to do. Should she tell the police? She now knew well that the police in this city where she had moved to had a problem with corruption. What if Mr. Rivers had bought them all, the way he would routinely buy politicians?

Should she call Rick? He was still asleep. Should she call Detective Atkinson? He had severed all ties with the police force, or so he said. She sat on her black leather couch, expensive designer bag at her feet, and gazed out the window at the bright afternoon sky. She was alone, and would have to fend for herself. She had escaped from the man she believed was her father on her own, and she had gotten a job to support herself on her own. But could she survive a hired killer on her own? She knew that when Mr. Rivers paid for something, he only bought the best.

Rick and his sister Alexandra had earlier planned to go down to After Dark and meet at dusk, along with Alex, who was late in coming. They sat next to each other and Leon turned on the laptop he had brought so that they could read the messages, "It's from someone named Josie," he said. "The lady who wrote the letter doesn't own a computer," nor did about half the vampires that he knew, and he figured it was because they had gone so long without one and probably didn't see them as any sort of necessity. "Josie wants to say hi to everyone. Here." he pushed the small computer toward them. "Go on. Read it."

Alexandra took it and pulled it close so she and Rick could view the screen. She scrolled down. "You ought to get yourself one of these;" she said, "catch up with the times, you know?"

"Nope," Rick said, "I don't need all that electronic junk. What would I use it for? My car is the only machine I need or want."

"Sell your art online, expand your business, have a website for your gallery, look at kittens." She began to read silently to herself, "They live in a very small town, a lot of farms, convenient with plenty of livestock . . . they're near a state forest, and surrounded by woods. It sounds like a perfect place to hide your existence from the world. It must be wonderful," she imagined out loud, "to not have to live in a city like this, with all the crime; just be hundreds of miles from nowhere. It must be a beautiful place."

"They must get blood straight from the cow, then." Alex arrived and came toward their table after helping himself from a tray. "And not have to rely on leftovers of uncertain quality from a slaughterhouse of uncertain cleanliness."

He pulled out a chair and sat next to Leon. "Are we sure this is a good idea? Communicating this way?"

"Why not?" Alexandra asked. "Everyone else does."

"The CIA could be reading this right now, you know," he said. "Or so they say."

"I've already sent her a message ahead of time to never type the V-word, Alex," Leon said. "That should just take care of any future problems."

"I wish we could go visit them," Alexandra whispered. "But it's so far away. We should send them something. Send them a gift, maybe. Because we can't just go out there and see them ourselves."

"This is wonderful." Rick stood up. "I've got to go open up the shop; gotta earn a living and all that." He took one last lingering look at the glow of the computer screen. "It's like a miracle, to find others of our kind, after so long." And then he drifted away.

When Rick arrived to open up the art gallery Rufus was behind the counter and Laura was talking to him; he seemed to be listening intently, whatever it was about.

"She got shot at," the boy said simply.

"What?"

"I got shot at." Her words echoed what Rufus already said.

"Okay," Rick said. "What the hell is going on?"

"Well, I was at the supermarket and I was putting stuff in my car and I dropped my keys, and when I bent to pick them up, bullets shot out the window of this big van that was parked behind my car. There was glass everywhere. I didn't see who did it. Whoever it was drove off in a hurry when he didn't get me."

He went to her and pulled her close. "Well, you're all right. You are all right, aren't you?"

"Yes. Well, I guess so," she said. "I didn't bother to go to the police. I don't trust the police in this town, not after finding out that Detective Atkinson's former partner turned out to be a serial killer. I just don't know what to do, Rick. It's my . . . it's Mr. Rivers. He's actually found me."

"We'll hide you," he said. "You can stay safe, with us, like you did last time you were in danger."

"Rick." she looked away. "I can't. If anything happened, I'd be responsible."

"What do you mean? Be responsible for what?"

"You know what they say about the factory that Mr. Rivers owned. He would rather blow it up than give in to the employees' demands for safer working conditions. If whoever he hired to come after me finds out where I'm staying, people are going to get hurt, not just me. I'm sorry, Rick. I can't stay with you, or with your family, or stay anywhere with anyone else you care about. It's just not safe." She got free of his embrace and picked her purse up off the countertop. "I'm sorry," she said again, walking toward the door.

"What are you going to do?"

"I don't know. I'll go home and lock the door. Maybe I'll push the couch up against the door, and pull the drapery so no one can see me through the windows."

"Do you think maybe he's just trying to scare you?" Rufus asked. "I mean, the guy missed, right? Maybe he missed on purpose, just to scare you, or something?"

"No, Rufus," she said sadly, "Mr. Rivers doesn't play games, unless he's sure he'll win." And then she was gone.

"We have to do something about this," Rick said quietly, watching her shut the door as she walked out.

"Do what?" Rufus asked. "What can we do?"

"I don't know, kid," he sighed. "Right now, I just don't know."

Laura sat alone in the darkness, on her bed, one dim lamp illuminating her room. She wished that Rick were with her. She had done as she said she would; she pushed the couch against the door, and drew the curtains so no one could see her through a window. She also turned out all the lights in her apartment, except for one to see by. She ate hastily prepared macaroni and cheese, the kind that came from a cardboard box, and some of it had dropped onto her silk dress. She didn't care; she had plenty of dresses. It wasn't her dress she was concerned about. She had only one life.

Again, she thought of how she wished that Rick were there with her. He would feel comfortable in the darkness, she knew. But it was best to keep him and everyone else she cared about far away. She had already learned that vampires were not as invincible as the legends about them told; a bullet to the head could kill him just as well as it could kill her.

In the morning, she would need to exit, and make her way cautiously to work. The inheritance left to her by her grandfather was not infinite. She had left the mansion that had begun to feel like a prison with only her favorite clothes and shoes and her mother's jewelry, and knowing her mother's father was wise enough to set up a fund for her that Mr. Rivers would not know about. Looking back, she realized her grandfather must have known what kind of man Mr. Rivers really was, and that she would need the money someday to escape his control and make a decent life for herself.

She startled when the landline phone in the living room rang. She got up to go answer it, carrying the bowl of macaroni with her.

"Laura, I got your message."

"Grandma? Oh thank God." She sat down on the Oriental rug so she would be near the floor in case more bullets flew in her direction through the windows, then she put the bowl of macaroni down on the floor to give her full attention to the call.

"I wanted to call, but I was at work. I do not want them to hear me, to find out I do know English after all. Listen, there is something I must tell you!"

"Grandma, someone tried to kill me today."

"What?"

"I was in a parking lot and someone took a shot at me, and if I hadn't dropped my car keys and bent down to pick them up,

I'd be dead. He shot out the windows of a van instead. I never saw who it was, either. The person just drove away when they didn't get me. I'm assuming it was a man, because those kinds of people Mr. Rivers hired, they were all men that I knew of."

"Mother of God, you've got to get away and hide somewhere. He knows where you are now."

"If I didn't let my picture get in that paper—" she sighed. "For the first time in my life, I was starting to be happy, and now this. I don't know what to do. I'm happy in this town. There are people I care about here. I don't want to just disappear again."

"Well, you might have to, my dear, for a while, anyway. Listen, I have not told you this, because when I met you, I was so excited, I forgot to tell you about it. But I clean the office that he has in his big house." To call the mansion a big house was an understatement. It was the size of a shopping mall, with multiple garages for his exotic cars, and behind the mansion were stables for his purebred horses. "But he is not always there, you know, he goes on business trips. He leaves his papers and things around. He has only me to clean up around there, no one else will he allow to clean in there. And I know why. Because he thinks I cannot read English. Mr. Rivers thinks I am stupid! Never mind, dear. Let me tell you this. He leaves papers around sometimes. And he writes notes to himself. When no one is around close by, I make a photocopy of something that looks important, I fold it up small, and put in my shoe, and keep cleaning all day, with the photocopy in my shoe. One by one, I take home papers. I have been doing this for a long time, and he does not know. I have enough now, enough to get him to go to jail. This is another reason I do not quit working for him, even though I cannot stand him."

"What's on the papers, Grandma?" She was curious now. She knew there were probably things that the Federal Bureau of Investigation would probably like to see, as well as things the

Securities and Exchange Commission would like to see, also. But she also knew he could buy his way out of trouble. "You know, he could just pay off anyone you send them to. You'd have to find someone who was a real do-gooder type, maybe, to get anywhere with that, I think."

"This is my plan, Laura. I will make many copies of the copies. I will not only send to FBI, I will send to newspapers, magazines, I will send all around. And I will not put my name on package, understand? This will be our secret! We tell no one. This way, my son and your mother will finally have justice! I will drive somewhere far away from where I live, and put them in postboxes. One by one, I will send them from different postboxes. It will be a big mystery who sent these things. No one will ever know, no one but you and me. And then they will know about the pollution that gets into drinking water, the sneaky investing, all those things he wants to keep quiet."

"Oh my God. You've got it all planned. What about the factory that blew up, Grandma? Did you find out anything about that?"

"One small paper has the date it happened on it, something about problems with labor relations, and then there is an amount of money written down. It's his handwriting. How much he paid for it to be done. These are things the government would like to know."

"I always knew he was a crook," Laura sighed. "And to think I grew up thinking he was my father."

"After my son died," she continued in her tired and sad voice, "I wanted to kill him myself. I wanted to kill him with my own hands. But I would just go to jail, and who would watch out for you? I work for him, many years. I keep my eyes open. I keep my mouth shut. When you are safe, that will be the time. You just need to be careful until I can do this."

They talked for hours. Laura began to feel the sadness of loss for not knowing her real family for so many years of her young life, all the missed birthdays and holidays, and wondered what her life would have been like if she grew up with what she now considered to be normal people. Normal working people who lived in normal houses and who didn't own mansions or yachts or private jets.

"There's so much I never knew, Grandma. I left home and I'm learning the world is not what I expected it would be." She couldn't tell her grandmother about all the things she discovered, of course, although she wished she could. "I've discovered some amazing things, I just can't begin to tell . . ." Her voice faded into silence when she realized there were things she had to keep to herself.

"Tell me about that nice young man, Laura! The artist! Tell me all about him."

"Well," *he's not that young*, she wanted to say, "he's very nice. Yes, he is." He doesn't go out during the day, and he drinks blood, sometimes he microwaves it, and sometimes he drinks it cold. "Well, yes, he's a real nice guy."

"How did you meet?"

"It's a really crazy story," she wanted to say, *I felt depressed and suicidal after growing up with Mr. Rivers for a father*, but she didn't. "I'm kind of embarrassed to tell it." *So I was trying to commit suicide, but I was too much of a coward, so went looking for a vampire to do it for me.* "I'll tell you some other time." *But he wouldn't go along with my plan.* "It's kind of silly, how we met, you know," *silly, like a dark tragic comedy.* "Sometimes I think my life has become a dark comedy," she said. "And now I have a hit man out to get me. I want to think if I can survive Mr. Rivers, I can survive anything. But now I'm not so sure about that. Not with bullets flying over my head."

Finally they hung up, and Laura turned out the lights again and decided to try to go back to bed, to try to sleep, hoping she would be alive in the morning.

Her cell phone rang now. It was in her purse, beside the bed. She snatched it up. "Who could this be now?" It was late, after one o'clock in the morning, "Hello?"

It was Leon. "Hi, how yah doin'?"

"Hi Leon," she yawned. "Look, I know you like to stay up late because you were brought up by vampires, and all, but I'm really tired."

"That's okay, I won't talk long. Just letting you know, Irina needs your help."

"She needs my help?" She was surprised. She had met Rick's mother once, but hadn't seen her or heard from her in a while. Irina was probably the oldest vampire in town, and the wealthiest. She owned a restaurant, a nightclub, rental units and real estate. "Why?"

"I think she wants you to do her a favor."

"What does she want me to do?"

"Deliver a package. That's all."

"Deliver a package?"

"Yeah, it's a long distance, and it's hard for them to travel; they might get exposed to daylight, and all that."

"Well, can't she just mail it? I don't mind, she's been very kind to me and everything, but, that's what most people do now."

"Well, she wants someone to make sure it gets there safely, and not get damaged, so she wanted me to find someone who can deliver it for her. She'll pay for the plane ticket, okay? And I'll drive you to the airport. You just have to take the box and get on the plane."

"Leon? How far away is this?"

"East coast."

Oh sheesh. "Does she need me to go over there to get it now?"

"No. Tomorrow night will be fine, Laura. Thanks!"

75

"Leon, I didn't say I would. I mean, can't I think about it?" And then it dawned on her; they were trying to send her far away.

"Sure. Call me tomorrow," he hung up.

Alexandra leaned against her desk in her small office and watched as Leon put the phone down. He had called Laura after getting off the phone with Rick and finding out about the attempted drive-by shooting. "Do you think this will work?" she asked.

"Hope so. We have to get her out of town somehow, and Rick says she won't let us just help her hide out somewhere like last time."

She looked at the cardboard box on the floor next to her desk. "Well, it's the only plan we have right now. She might not even want to do it. She might even figure out why we're sending her."

"This had better work, or she could be dead soon," he said.

"There's one thing we forgot to do."

"What?" he asked.

"You told her I want her to do what?" Irina sat behind the massive antique dark mahogany wooden desk, demanding to know what was going on. "You just got off the phone with that girl, and you told her that I want her to deliver something to the East Coast? And you have taken my fine silver drinking vessels? That I've kept for so long?"

"You haven't used them in over a hundred years," Alexandra stated simply. "We figured you wouldn't miss them."

"Look," Leon broke in, and he gave Irina his best rehearsed sad lost puppy dog look, "it's probably the only way to protect her. She has to get out of town. Someone tried to shoot her, but he missed. She won't let us just hide her somewhere. We needed an excuse to get her out of town."

"You, Leon, have been a bad influence on my daughter." Her several diamond bracelets and large garnet ring flashed in the dim light as she pointed her pale thin finger at him.

"It was my idea to take the silver cups," Alexandra said.

"Never mind! If I did not love you two children I would hurl you both out the window! And I am supposed to pay for her ticket?" she snarled. "Or have I done so already?"

"No, I was going to take care of that tomorrow night," said Alexandra.

"Fine, then go ahead. Take them! And I do not want to hear of this again," she sighed. "Why I put up with this, I do not know."

They walked out of Irina's office together; Leon followed Alexandra down the long dimly lit hallway. He briefly considered turning back and saying thank you, but decided it would be better to silently walk out and to keep walking. He followed Alexandra into the stairwell, and the two of them began to descend to the floor below. They stopped before opening the door to the next level and she said, "Don't worry. She'll only be mad at us for a few centuries. Then she'll get over it."

They both laughed out loud, and Leon wondered if they could be heard by those on the floor above. They continued back towards Alexandra's office. "Well," she said, "I have to finish the balancing the books, and all that."

"Yeah," he said, "I gotta get back to work, too."

"I'm not so sure if this is going to be a good idea, after all." She then said suddenly, drifting back into her office and sitting back down at her desk. "We're sending someone they don't know, to deliver this, and we're sending them a gift because we have a motive."

"Our motive," he said, remaining out in the hallway, "is saving Laura. Look, she's going to get on a plane in a few days, or sooner, as soon as she can get packed. What could go wrong?"

"I don't know, Leon. I just don't know if we're doing the right thing."

Just then the phone on Alexandra's desk rang; she answered it, "Yes? Okay" She sighed and hung up. "She wants to see me. Now. Just me."

"What now?"

"I don't know," she said. "Maybe she's decided to hurl me out the window after all." She got up to go back upstairs. "Don't worry. She probably just wants to yell some more, or something."

He stood and watched her go. "See yah later."

Alexandra wandered slowly back into Irina's office. "Yes, mother?" she said quietly, and waited for the rest of her irate commentary.

"Sit down," Irina said, pointing at a soft cushioned antique chair. "Sit and I will tell you what is so special about those old silver cups."

So she sat to listen. "You're right. I should have asked. I just didn't think you'd care about them. They've been put away in storage for so long."

"They've been in storage because I can't look at them. Alexa," Irina began, "do you remember how your father was killed? When you were just a child?"

"Yes." How could she ever forget. "I remember how you found him," *with a stake pounded into him.* "You told us that. And then you hunted down the men who did it, and you got them alone, one by one," *and she gave them no mercy.* She remembered how it was all told to her. And then their village was destroyed, so they decided to leave, to go to America, and try to start over.

"The cowards not only murdered your father, Alexa, they stole things from our house. Finally, when I caught up with the last of the men, I found those. I did not even notice them missing, until I saw them on his shelf, after I was done finishing him. And so I took them back and brought them with us. They were your father's. They're very ancient; older than me, older than your father was when they murdered him, and older than his father. That's why I put them away. I can't look at them. It just makes me sad to look at them. I did not tell my children all the unnecessary details. It's just all too sad to remember these things. And I was never proud of myself, for getting revenge. But I couldn't shame your father's memory by letting them get away with it. We like to say we came to this country because of the revolution, like so many others did then. But that wasn't the real reason." She reached to remove her diamond necklace, then the matching earrings; she took them off and put them on her desk. "I won't see Rick unhappy if something happens to that girl. Send this instead. It's not old, but it's much more valuable. And then maybe they won't mind harboring this little refugee."

Josephine handed the printout of the most recent email to Annasophia, and so she sat down in a soft chair by the fire to read it. They intended to send to her a small gift along with their greetings from far away. "They don't need to send anything. Tell them that knowing they are out there, knowing that others of our kind survive somewhere; that is enough." She handed back the printed message. "This is like a dream come true, Josie, to find them. If we didn't let Muriel go ahead and write that story last year and let her publish it, we would never know about them. It was meant to happen like this, somehow, that Ben's niece would bring this about. By why are they sending someone all the way to deliver, when they could just put it in a box and send it?"

Josie sat down on the couch next to Sophie's grey cat. "They say this girl has some kind of thug problem in her life right now, so they need an excuse to get her out of town for a while. I'll tell her about the motel where Sharona stayed. We can meet her there or at the truck stop and then bring her to see you. She can tell us all about everyone out there."

"I'll have to find something to send back, then, when she goes home. It wouldn't be proper not to," Sophie sighed. "Or, if she does go home, since as you say, she has a problem. But I don't think people from California will be much impressed with our very small town." She stood up to put another small log on the fire; the small house did have a modern heating system, but she preferred the warmth and comfort of a natural blaze.

"I've never met anyone from California," Josie said, realizing she hadn't met many people from far away unless they were truck drivers travelling through. "I bet she's blonde and pretty and sophisticated, and all that. You're right. She probably won't be very impressed by us. She probably won't like the weather here, either. I would bet she's never seen snow."

"If we're having a visitor, I suppose I'll have to clean this place up, then," Sophie said as she looked around. There were two sewing machines on different tables, one old and one new, bolts of different fabrics and scraps of velvet and lace strewn about, as she used her living room as a work area most of the time. There were also several old fashion magazines from the 1930's and 1940's, which she had kept since they were new, and from which she got ideas for her supposedly new creations. "I will have to move all these things into storage when she comes to visit, and then take them all back out again."

"Why move everything, Sophie? This is what you do; you're a dressmaker. There is nothing wrong with that."

"The place is a mess, Josie. I'm surprised I can find anything. I will have to be a decent hostess. It would be rude of us to let her stay at the motel, of course, but she might not be happy to stay here. Who would keep her company during the day?"

"We can ask Muriel. She's renting out rooms."

"But that's not fair to Muriel, and it would be unkind to expect this visitor to pay for a room when she is a guest."

"Well, let me ask," Josie suggested. "I'll find out."

"And tell me, how is the new girl doing? Sharona?"

"The manager likes her. He said he'd give her more hours there. She was happy; she said she would try to save up some money now to go to school, but she doesn't know what she wants to do yet. She needs to finish her high school diploma first. Muriel is glad to have her, too. She helps clean up around the place sometimes, Muriel says. And she doesn't mind that Sharona is a werewolf. I guess Muriel was just kind of shocked to know werewolves exist. Well, I was too. But she's probably used to things like this by now, with her neighbors being vampires and all that. So I guess she's like, okay, so she's a werewolf, so whatever."

Sophie nodded in agreement. "That's good. It looks like she's found a good place to stay, then, after all the troubles she's been through. She needs to be near people who can understand her somewhat unusual situation."

"I did find some other things out," Josie continued. "We hung around in the back parking lot after work, just talking and stuff. No one else was around to hear, so she told me some things. Now we know what the thing is with werewolves and the full moon, because I asked her about that. She said it helps to stare at it while concentrating, meditating, something like that. It makes it easier for her, when there's a full moon. She also says psychic energy is stronger when there's a full moon, but she doesn't know why that is. Although she can transform herself—that's what she called it—almost any time she wants to now. She just needs to be somewhere quiet, preferably alone."

"I see. Well, that's how legends are born, as we know. There is always a little truth in every myth. We already knew that."

She put down the printout and picked up her embroidery and went back to working on it.

"She told me they—I mean people like her and her grandparents—they practiced a lot of self-discipline and self-denial to achieve the higher mindset needed to make them able to do these things. They didn't believe in accumulating a lot of material things; they lived very simply. People who became werewolves used to go out alone into the forest and live off only what the forest provided, but then they would come back to the village and bring back what they learned from nature." Josie reached to run her hand through the cat's fur; the cat opened her eyes and yawned. "And you know what else she said?"

"What?" Sophie asked, not looking up, as she concentrated on her work.

"She said it's true about legends having a little truth in them. You know the story 'Little Red Riding Hood?' She said that today people think it's just a made-up story to scare kids away from going into the woods or talking to strangers. But it's not. She said, 'how do you think it is that the wolf eats the girl, then when the hunter slices open the wolf, the girl comes out alive and whole again?' I said, 'I don't know.' Then I realized, yeah, that is pretty strange, even for a fairy tale. So then she explained, the story was told so people would remember the old ways. The grandmother is Mother Earth, and the girl is on a journey into the spirit world, to grandmother's house in the woods, because it's easier to connect to the spirit world out in the wilderness. She meets the wolf, in grandmother's bed, because to walk into the spirit world, you need to go into a dream state, as if you were sleeping. In the story the wolf eats the girl, but the real meaning, she said, is that her spirit has taken the shape of a wolf; it's as if your mind is inside of a wolf. The hunter is the one teaching her these things. He helps her come out of the wolf and back into the world of the living. Being inside the wolf is like walking into the spirit world."

Sophie looked up and stopped stitching. "This girl amazes me, even with the long life I have lived and all that I have seen. You can also see she is a part of a history that has almost been done away with because of people's wanton ignorance; and how sad, to be remembered only in fairy tales." She picked up the printed email again and looked at it briefly. "If there are more people like us, I wonder if maybe she is not the last of her kind, also?"

"I don't know, but I'm glad she came here. The pig that used to bother us, he never came back."

"Did she say where her people are from? Originally?" Sophie was curious.

"She said something about her family originally being from a place called Livonia, but I don't know where that is."

"Near Lithuania, I think. I recall there were many legends of werewolves in Livonia." Sophie sighed again and went back to the original subject. "Well, I hope this does not turn into some sort of disaster, when this person comes all the way out to visit us. We do want to make a decent impression."

"Of course not," Josie said. "She'll come and visit and meet everyone and see the farms and see the cows and horses and we can show her the farm stand and drive her around to see the lake with the moon over it at night, when it's all so pretty. It's not much to see, but that's what we have to show her."

Sophie smiled and said, "Let's make sure we don't show her the run-down shacks by the lake with the junk cars parked in front of them. Especially the one with the piles of beer cans stacked up on the front porch. That wouldn't be very pretty, would it? And we mustn't let her see the old barn in the woods where the kids make drugs and get themselves almost blown up. Karl has been telling me all sorts of things that go on in this innocent little town all around us that we don't know about."

Josie laughed, "No, we won't take her to see those places," and added, "Well, anyway, what could possibly go wrong?"

Rufus was leaning over the counter next to the cash register in the gallery when Laura walked in. "Where is he?"

"He's upstairs," he said simply, wondering why she was so direct this time. She seemed slightly upset somehow, and he wondered if she had been shot at again.

But just then Rick was coming down the stairs on his own. "Laura? You're okay? Nothing else happened? Did it?"

She looked at him with sadness in her eyes. "Was it your idea? To send me away?" she asked.

"Send you away? What the hell are you talking about?"

Rufus realized the conversation was going to get serious and so he drifted back upstairs to force himself to try and study.

"Well, Leon called my cell phone late last night," and then she hastily explained everything as fast as she could.

"Well, that's typical," Rick said. "Leon is always getting involved in everyone else's damn business. I'll just call him and tell him to knock it off."

"No. I think he might be right. It's the only way. He's found me. If I don't get out of here, I could be killed, along with people I care about. You don't know what he can do, Rick. I think Leon might be right."

"Are you sure?"

"No. I'm not sure. Since I came here, for the first time in my life, I've been happy. I don't want to go, Rick. But maybe I have to. I'll try to come back when it's safe, if I can. But I'm not going to get on a plane. That's what he'll expect me to do. I'm not going to risk that. How did he know I was at the supermarket? I'm wondering if my cell phone might have been bugged, or hacked, or whatever it is they do."

He looked directly at her, wondering if she was just being paranoid. "You think he could do that?"

"He couldn't, but he can hire people to do it for him. I left my phone at my apartment. I'll get another one, a new one that

84

hasn't been touched by anyone yet. I'll use my cell phone one more time to tell people I'm on my way to the airport. And then I'll get in my car and go. I have to do this alone, Rick."

He looked at her and exhaled slowly, almost like a sigh. "It's a very long way to go. You haven't been driving very long. You know I'd go with you if I could. Do you really want to do that?"

She shook her head slowly "Rick, I can't get on a plane. If he finds out . . . I'd worry that something could happen to the plane because of me. All those people. I dread what could happen if I got on a plane. Besides, he won't expect me to be brave enough to drive across country. He would have people looking for me at the airport."

Suddenly, Rick looked away from her and looked up to gaze out through the window that faced the street. She kept talking, but she then realized he was no longer listening. "Rick?"

He quickly took hold of her, threw her to the ground, holding her head down towards the floor . . .

"What are you doing?" she screamed, never having seen him move so fast before, almost with lightning speed. For a brief moment, she imagined he had suddenly turned predatory. Images from horror movies that terrified her as a little girl came up from being buried deep in her subconscious mind.

But then the window exploded inwards. Glass flew into the art gallery, covering the carpet, destroying assorted paintings that faced the window, with sharp edges landing inches away from her face. She then heard the wail of tires shriek against pavement outside.

"He's gone," Rick said, and then he helped her back up and brushed some glass from out of her hair.

"Oh my God," she gasped. "That's exactly what happened at the parking lot." She turned to stare at the shot out window.

"What's going on?" It was Rufus, charging back down the stairs to check out what the commotion was. "Whoa!" He saw the broken glass and the destroyed window.

"Another drive by, kid," Rick said, holding on to Laura while she stared silently in shock at the damage. "Didn't I already tell you it helps to be able to see in the dark?"

"Thank God you can see in the dark," she whispered. "Oh Rick, I'm sorry."

"It's just a window. It can be fixed."

"No . . . for what I thought."

"What?" He held her close to stop her from shaking.

"Never mind."

Rufus fetched a broom and Rick began to sweep up the glass from the carpet. Laura asked if she could help and Rick said, "No. Don't worry. We'll take care of it."

He then went on about the nuisance of having to file an insurance claim for the damages, and hoped that Leon or someone else could locate a piece of plywood from the rubbish in the alleyway large enough to board up the window until repairs could be properly made. When almost all of the shards of glass were in a pile to be more easily disposed of, Rick looked up to notice the bullet holes in the wall near where they both had been standing before it happened. "What the hell is this town coming to? It's getting worse than a damn city."

Someone on the street who witnessed the incident called the police, and soon they saw the flashing lights of a cruiser arriving in front of the gallery.

"Don't tell them, Rick. I don't want them to know it was meant for me," she whispered before they came in.

When the officers came through the door, Rick looked at them and said, "Hey! Some people just don't appreciate art."

Finally after what seemed like too long a time, and after taking statements from all three of them, the policemen left. Rick told the police that the window was shot out by someone in a car that was parked on the street outside, and they did not know who could have done it, and basically that was the truth. Rufus did not have to say much because he was not present when it happened; he only came down to see the aftermath. And Laura simply added, "If he didn't knock me down and out of the way . . ."

As to the possible motive, that was left out.

After the police finally left, Rick told Rufus to keep an eye on Laura while he went to her apartment to gather a few of her things so she could stay the night and not have to be alone. She remained upstairs above the gallery, and did her best to stay away from the windows. Rufus tried unsuccessfully to make small talk with her, but she remained in a state of mild shock and despair. She sat at the small kitchen table, taking an occasional sip from the cup of tea Rick had brewed for her before he left.

"You mind?" Rufus said as he put a mug in the microwave.

"What? Oh, no, of course not," she said quietly, not looking at him; instead she simply stared down at the teabag in her cup.

"I guess you're used to seeing stuff like this, right?"

"Yes, of course. I suppose I am by now." And then she said, "I just can't understand why he hates me so!"

"I don't know either," Rufus said. He pulled out a chair after the bell on the microwave chimed, and sat across from her. "I don't know, Miss Rivers, I just don't know. I hope you'll be okay. I mean, you know, I hope you'll be able to get away."

"I don't want to go, but I have to," she sighed; and then she looked directly at him. "If I stay here, he'll hunt me down, and other people could get hurt, too."

Rufus heard voices downstairs and hurriedly finished the contents of his mug and put it in the sink. "I'll go see what's going on."

He went down and saw Rick standing there with a tote bag taken from Laura's apartment while he was pointing out the damage to Justina.

She turned and saw Rufus. "I saw the police cars go down the street and stop here, so I knew something was wrong. How are you Rufus?"

"Oh, hi again. Yeah. It's a big mess. A drive by, I guess."

Two more people walked in, Rick's brother Alex and a few others Rufus had not met before. One of them carried in some large pieces of thin plywood and another held a roll of duct tape. The one with the duct tape said, "This won't hold very well, but it's all we could find on short notice."

"Nice to see yah again," Rufus said to Justina. "I think I'd better go back up and see if she's still okay."

"Here," Rick said, and handed him the tote bag, "bring this upstairs with you."

"Okay." Rufus drifted back up the stairs, and Laura asked what was going on.

"They're just trying to board up the window, that's all," he said. "Looks like seeing the police car is going to bring every vampire in the neighborhood over here."

"Oh," she said, finally sounding a little more relaxed. "Is that all? I thought it was more trouble."

She stayed the rest of the night, and the curtains in Rick's home above the art gallery were drawn so that no one could see inside. The lights were mostly kept shut off to make it even more difficult for anyone outside to see movement or activity in the upper level of the house. Rick went out and came back with some takeout for her. "I don't know if you like fried chicken," he said. "It's what I used to bring the kids who came here with Rufus, before, you know, they had to go away for a while," meaning the boys had gotten themselves arrested. "The place is just around the corner, and the food doesn't smell as bad as some of the fast food places around here."

She thanked him and ate at the kitchen table in the semidarkness. "I'll eat anything right now."

He sat across from her after taking his own mug out of the microwave. "You know, before you go on your trip," he began, "maybe you ought to consider dressing a little differently when you travel?"

She suddenly looked away from her food and looked at him. "What's wrong with the way I dress?"

"Nothing," he said, "but you just obviously look wealthy wherever you go, whatever you do. Quite frankly, you just look rich, Laura. Maybe you should get some different clothes;" he paused, "you know, be less noticeable."

"I guess most girls don't wear Italian heels and diamond earrings and pearls these days," she admitted. "But it's what I'm used to."

"Most girls don't carry a two thousand dollar Italian purse, either. Do you even own a pair of blue jeans?"

"Well . . . not a pair of cheap ones, no. And the purse was only fifteen hundred. Do you think I should leave this ring behind?" She looked down at it; it was a large pink sapphire surrounded with diamonds. "It was my mother's. I'd really miss it."

"You know, before I met you, I never even knew sapphires came in colors like that. But if you wear cheap looking clothes with a ring like that, people will probably think it's fake. In fact, if I didn't know, I would think a stone that big was artificial. It's so beautiful, it almost can't be real."

"At least I can keep this, then." And she continued eating, realizing she was famished. "I feel all of a sudden I don't even know who I am anymore. Maybe I never knew who I was. Being Laura Rivers was all just a bad dream. But who am I, Rick? I just don't know anymore."

He looked at her and inhaled. "If you can get away, again, this time, then that will be up to you, won't it?"

"I have to stop using his last name, I know that. It will be hard to get used to, though. Every time someone asks my name, am I going to hesitate before I answer?"

"Maybe if you start calling yourself Laura Blasko from this day on, you'll get used to it?"

She tossed the last chicken bone back into the greasy package and put her head down on the table. "I don't know. Oh my God, I don't want to have to leave everything I know, and start all over, again. I hope I can come back, when it's finally safe."

"I hope you can, too." He got up and put the empty mug in the sink next to the one that was already there. "Well, if you're going to be going alone, you'll need to blend in, fade into the background, so no one will notice you, or remember seeing you. It's too late to get another car, but if you park it away from whatever building you go into, people might not notice the BMW. Have you thought about changing your hair? I mean, just so you don't look like you?" They talked for several more hours and the night wore on. Finally, exhausted, she went to bed. After he was sure she that was asleep, Rick picked up the phone and started making phone calls.

". . . She says she's a size six."

Sergeant Stepanek sat at his desk in the small police station and worked his way slowly through the dullness of routine paperwork. He looked up to gaze out the window and saw flurries of light snow fluttering rapidly through the cold night wind. Soon the spring would finally come, and the remaining snow would melt and the frozen ground would begin to thaw. His eyes went back to the paperwork until he heard the door open; someone was coming in. He recognized the sound of the heavy footsteps. It was the man who reported the wolf attack at the truck stop, in addition to being involved in various other incidents and misdemeanors over the many years. Karl had recollections of him being drunk and disorderly and other assorted miscellaneous troubles.

He put the lid over the large ceramic mug that was next to the stack of papers on his desk and looked up to see the visitor. "What's up, Gary?"

It was hard not to recognize Gary Curran. He was slightly above six feet tall, and obese. Often during this type of weather he wore a fake fur lined trapper hat, grey sweat pants, a fake black leather jacket—probably in a failed attempt to look cool—and orange knitted acrylic mittens.

"Just wanted to talk to yah, Sarge."

"Oh, that's fine, Gary. Sit yourself down. It's a slow night."

And so Gary sat down in a chair that seemed too small to hold his weight but somehow it did; he seemed hesitant to talk.

"What brings you out on this cold night, Gary?" the Sergeant asked, encouraging him to begin. "Something you need to report?"

"It's about that wolf, Sarge."

"You ever see that animal again, Gary?"

"Well, no. Nope. I haven't. Never saw it again, Sarge."

"Then what is this about? The wolf is probably gone. We have real criminals to worry about, you know."

"Well, Sarge, there was something mighty strange about that wolf that I saw."

"What was strange about it?"

"Well, it was there, and it went after me, but when I saw it, it looked almost, sort of, you know, transparent."

"Transparent, Gary?"

"Yeah. You know, transparent. Like it was a ghost wolf. It was there, I could see it clear as day, but it didn't look completely solid."

"Well, I don't know what to make of something like that. As far as I could see on the night of the incident, you weren't injured. Are you sure you're okay? I mean, really, are you okay?" he stressed the word 'okay.'

"Oh, yeah, I'm fine. I just wanted to tell you what was so strange about that wolf, Sarge. I mean, I've never seen anything like it in my whole life." Gary looked directly at Karl Stepanek. "Do you believe in strange things?"

"Believing in strange things is not part of my job, but every once in a while, someone calls the station to report a flying saucer. I drive down to check it out, and it usually turns out to be just kids who were smoking dope and thought they saw a few other things, too." Karl maintained his serious expression the best he could. "Sometimes folks call in about Bigfoot. Never heard of a transparent wolf, though. That's a new one. Is that all, or is there anything else?"

"Well, Sarge, it's just, you know, there's all kinds of legends in this town."

"Legends about what?" He went back to shuffling through his papers, hoping it would encourage the man to leave. In the background, the radio made occasional noise and static, but the volume was kept peacefully low.

"Don't you hear all the stories? You work the night shift. How long have you been in this town?" Gary demanded in his usual annoying voice.

"Probably a lot longer than you have, Gary, and I don't know what stories you're referring to. I really don't," Karl insisted.

"You don't?" His voice suddenly became shrill, "There are legends of vampires in this town, Sarge!"

Sergeant Stepanek flung the papers down on the desk in frustration. "Gary! This police force is underpaid, underequipped, and understaffed. We are running around trying to catch people before they blow up another building while cooking drugs; and these same people are starting their own small town crime wave. We are trying to keep the tramps and vagrants from setting up camps in the woods so they can live there. We are trying to keep drunks off the main road all night long. And we don't have the capacity to deal with transparent wolves. And if you harass anyone or cause any trouble for people thinking that they are vampires, then I am going to have to bring you in."

"Sorry to bother you, Sarge." He got up, about to leave.

"No, now sit down, Gary. I'm not done talking to you."

Gary sat down again, looking back at the Sergeant warily.

"Now, Gary," he said slowly, as if speaking to a child, "you know how much I like you," Karl lied, "and I am trying to help you. Do you think seeing this apparition could have anything to do with feelings of guilt?"

"I'm not guilty of anything, Sarge!"

"No, not of any crime. That's not what I mean. Look, you don't do this job for as long as I have without learning something about human nature. I've been hearing things from some of the girls that work down at that truck stop. They say you're a little too friendly sometimes. Some of those girls think you're getting kind of fresh. Maybe this wolf thing is just your subconscious telling you something?"

Gary got up from his seat again. "I'll see yah, Sarge."

"Take it easy, Gary. Come again if you have anything serious to report."

He watched the heavily built man shuffle slowly out the door, and looked through the window to see his truck drive away. "Idiot." He lifted the lid off his mug and took a sip. "Damn it. It's gone cold." He would have to reheat it in the barely functioning microwave that was in the station breakroom. "Nothing worse than cold blood on a miserable night like this."

Sharona and Josephine had come to Annasophia's house to help package orders that were to be shipped out to people who had made purchases online. When they arrived she was finishing up a telephone call. "Thank you, Karl, for taking care

93

of it, and for letting me know." She put the phone down and went into the living room where the girls were getting ready to pack things. "I'm glad you thought of this, Josie," Sophie said, referring to the new website. "Not as many people stop by the store these days."

"She has a dress shop with another lady," Josie explained to Sharona. "The other lady works there during the day, and Sophie comes by at night to pick up repairs and orders that are left for her to do."

"Oh, that's smart," Sharona said. "Run a business with someone who can work during the day."

"And she teaches sewing classes in a back room at the dress shop at night sometimes." Josie carefully folded the mauve colored gown and wrapped it in tissue paper before putting it in the box. "Can you believe someone would pay a thousand dollars for a dress?"

"It's beautiful," Sharona said. "I wish I had a dress like that." She sat on the floor taping the boxes shut because the couch was covered with dresses that were soon to be sent out.

"I shall make one for you, then," Sophie offered.

"But where would I wear it?"

"There aren't many fancy places out here in the boondocks." Josie sat next to her on the braided rug and taped an address label onto the box. "But maybe if you go back to school, you would need a nice dress for a prom, or graduation, or something."

"Well, maybe," she said. "Yes, that would be nice, if I can finish school, I'd have something nice to wear under those silly robes they make people graduate in."

"Then that is what I shall do," Sophie said. "When you are ready to finish school, Sharona, you shall have a nice dress to wear."

"You would do that for me? Oh, thank you; that would be so nice of you. Well, I guess then that means I really do have to finish school now, instead of just talking about it."

Sophie smiled and watched the two girls while they worked. "Now, then, the other thing we wanted to talk about?"

"Well," Sharona began hesitantly, "I think the main reason you haven't seen or heard him . . . I mean, Ben's ghost, is because he seems to believe you might blame him for something that happened long ago."

Josie looked at Sharona in amazement. "You've been talking to the Professor?"

"Well, he talks to me, so . . . yeah."

Sophie was silent a moment. "Oh no, how could I blame him."

"He wouldn't say what it was, though." Sharona continued on with her work.

"A long time ago, Ben made a small mistake. We both did," she sighed. "Because of that, someone found out about us, and some of us were killed. But I never blamed him. Oh no, I never blamed Ben for any of it." She went back to reviewing the printed out orders, holding the paper in front of her face so neither of the girls would see the sadness that suddenly welled up in her eyes.

"He says you probably still also have a crush on this other person."

"Sharona?" Sophie asked. "What other person does Ben think I could still have any interest in?"

"Someone named Douglas, I think."

"I never knew any Douglas."

"He gave a last name . . . I'm trying to remember . . . Douglas Fairbanks. Yeah. The professor said he wonders if you still have a crush on this guy Douglas Fairbanks."

"You never mentioned anyone named Douglas, Sophie, that I can remember," Josie said. "Was he someone who had a farm around here once?"

"Girls!" Sophie sat down in the big soft chair and looked as if she might laugh but then seemed sad again. "Douglas Fairbanks was a movie star that every girl had a crush on a very long time ago."

"He was?" Josie asked. "Never heard of him."

"Of course you've never heard of him, dear, he's probably been dead as long as Ben has. I can't believe Ben is still fussing that I had a crush on Douglas Fairbanks, just like any girl did back then. After being dead all these decades, he's still going on about Douglas Fairbanks?"

"Well," Sharona laughed, "I think most ghosts are kind of stuck in the past about stuff like that."

Sophie looked up at the ceiling, her memory drifting back into happier times. "Ben used to tease me mercilessly about that foolish Douglas Fairbanks. I would have to say, 'I would never have a chance with Mr. Fairbanks, he's already married.' And Ben would say, 'you don't know, if he met you and saw how pretty you are, he might just leave Mary Pickford.' And we would both laugh."

"Who was Mary Pickford?" Josie asked.

"Don't either of you girls ever watch old movies? I suppose not. Mary Pickford was another movie star, very beautiful, very rich and famous. Together they were like Hollywood royalty. And those were the days when they had class, not like the useless and foolish celebrities you see today. And then we found out that Douglas Fairbanks and Mary Pickford broke up, and he would say, 'Now maybe you'll have a chance.' And I would laugh and tell him to just shut up. And then we started to make plans to marry. But he got killed when someone found out about us, when someone found out about his involvement with vampires. And my dreams were destroyed, along with some innocent people's lives. You girls are lucky today. Most people don't believe in vampires or werewolves. It gives you a little bit of safety. But back then, even in the early part of the twentieth century, even in America, where we came to get away from ignorance, even then, in this what we thought would be the land of enlightenment . . . if they found out about you, they would kill you."

Sharona and Josephine looked at each other grimly.

"She's right," Sharona said. "Look at what happened to my grandparents."

Josephine said nothing and continued to work. She got up to reach for another dress to package up, and began to wrap it in tissue paper.

"Never mind, girls," Sophie said. "This is too depressing. We shall change the subject. Sharona, do you know what you want to do after you finish school?"

"No," she said quietly. "Actually, right now, I have no idea what I want to do with my life. I just know I have to do something. And to do something, I guess I need to go to school. Being a werewolf is cool and all that. I can wander around and get to know the spirits around here. There are a lot of them. There's an old Native American in the forest near the lake. He talks to me sometimes. He says, 'Greetings, noble spirit wolf.' Then he talks on and on. He speaks English well enough to understand. He must have learned it long ago when he was alive. I'm probably the only one who's listened to him in like a few centuries. He complains that the white man took his land and burned his village. I don't even know his name yet, but he seems okay. Then there is this hitchhiker who got run over by a car a long time ago. I can tell it was a long time ago because he looks like a hippie or something. I think he was smoking pot when he got killed, because he seems like he's still stoned. And he's still standing out by the road that leads up onto the highway, waiting for someone to pick him up and take him somewhere that he'll never get to. It's kind of sad. Most people can't see him so no one else knows that he's there. It's like he's forever stoned and waiting for someone to stop their car and pick him up and take him away from there. He must have been so stoned when he got killed; he doesn't even know he's dead. He saw me and thought I was his long lost dog that he had when he was a kid. I'll go back out as myself rather than a wolf later, so I can try to talk to him and straighten him out. But I don't know if I can get through to him, because he's so out of it. There are a lot of spirits out there who just have no one to listen to them about the problems that they had when they were alive and that they are still all worked up about, or the problems that they have now that they're dead. Plus there are also these assorted forest spirits that you can see when you're walking on the other side; they don't communicate much. People would be surprised that there are so many beings out there that you don't normally see unless you're in an altered state. It's almost always a new discovery of some kind, over there. But this kind of stuff doesn't pay the bills, so some day I'm going to have to figure out what to do to earn a living. Being a waitress is okay for now, but I want to go to school for something. I just don't know what."

"Maybe you can be a medium, or something," Josie suggested. She reached to caress Sophie's cat, as she had suddenly appeared out from under the pile of gowns to sit on the rug next to them.

"Oh no, we never believed in taking money for this," Sharona quietly insisted. "We just don't."

"She's right, Josephine," Sophie said. "Besides, she'll need something steady and dependable. It is just a sad reality of life, girls, that we can't all devote our lives to doing the things we enjoy."

"Don't you enjoy sewing and making things, Sophie?" Josie asked, and she got up to fetch another gown off the couch and get it ready to send out.

"Well, yes, but to earn enough to pay the bills I need to work faster than I would like to. When orders come in I have to get them done on time to deliver," she said. "Oh well. I do usually enjoy designing beautiful things and I can run my own business. But if not enough people buy them, then I don't earn enough." And then she gazed intently down at the both of them. "Will someone please tell me why vampires are supposed to all be rich?"

"Because the ones on TV all live in castles?" Sharona suggested.

"Well, real life isn't like TV," Josie said. "If we were rich, we wouldn't have to worry about customers at the truck stop bothering us while we're trying to work. But the pig never came back, so that's a relief."

Laura did not recognize herself in the bathroom mirror. She ran her fingers through her hair—her new hair—and pulled at her dark bangs; she had never had bangs before, "Is all this really necessary?" she asked Rick, as he stood in the background watching her disappointment.

"If I can't recognize you, then the hit man your father hired probably won't, either. He'll be looking for a blonde. An expensive blonde."

She looked down and saw that there was still residue of hair dye around the sink, no matter how much they had tried to clean it. Irina had sent over her personal hairdresser with instructions to change Laura's appearance as much as possible. Now she was a brunette, with a pageboy style haircut. And worse, she wore faded blue jeans, sneakers, and a gray sweatshirt, things that Justina, a friend of Rick's whom she had just met, picked out and brought for her, along with a purse that was made of different colored leather patches stitched together. To her it all looked so plain, so common . . . she looked at herself and saw another person she could not recognize. And then, suddenly, she realized who this person was: It was Laura Blasko. She was looking in the mirror at who she had become. Laura Blasko. She repeated the name over and over silently to herself, whispered it to herself in her mind. This is what Laura Blasko looks like.

Laura Rivers was gone and nowhere to be found.

"You look like Imogene Coca," Justina laughed quietly. She was hanging around in the hallway outside the bathroom. Rufus told Laura that she had come in before, but she had not seen her. It was right after the window was shot out, she was told.

"Who is this Imogene person?" she asked. "Do we know this lady, Miss Coca?"

"You don't know her, but we remember her," Rick said quietly, staring at her. "She was an actress in the 1950's with a hairdo like that. And yes, you do look like her. Sort of."

"Oh, well, then at least I look like someone glamorous, I guess. Was this Imogene pretty?"

"Yes, she was," Rick said.

"Oh come on," Justina said. "It's not that bad. You just look like everyone else now. That's how you have to look if you don't want anyone to find you."

"If he finds me, he will kill me." She finally turned and looked at them both. They were gazing at her like she was this new person that had suddenly arrived from nowhere, "And maybe other people, too. I don't know why he's like that, but he is."

"You're sure you don't want to stay and hide somewhere?" Rick asked again, leaning against the wall across from the door to the bathroom.

"I do want to stay, but what would happen if I did? We already talked about this." She was determined, and almost ready to go. Leon had come over earlier during the day and brought her a new cell phone along with a GPS to help find her destination. Both were out of the box, and never touched by anyone. She would leave her old cell phone back at her apartment, in case her movements were being tracked through her phone. She had new clothes—casual clothes—in an old battered second hand suitcase. She would bring one good outfit for when she met the people she was going to meet, to make her delivery. There was only one more thing they were waiting for. "So," she asked, finally stepping out of the bathroom, "what is this thing I'm supposed to deliver, as an excuse to get me out of town?"

"My sister will bring it over soon," Rick said. "I'm going to drive behind your car down the road for a while, to make sure no one is following your car. I won't be able to go very far." If the sky began to brighten, he would be useless, and they both knew it. "If I could go with you, I would." It was already decided she would drive out at night; the hit man would not expect her to take off for parts unknown at midnight. All conversations over her cell phone—her old cell phone—indicated that she was being driven to the airport first thing in the morning to board a plane headed for Mexico.

"I have to go, you guys," Justina said. "Laura, good luck." And she gave her a quick hug. "I don't know what this is all about, you having a hit man after you and all that, but be safe. Don't get caught." She left.

Laura heard Justina exchange a few words with Rufus, who was watching television, and then heard her light footsteps going down to the lower floor and then out the door.

"Your friend seems nice."

"Yeah, she is. Well," he inhaled, and then let it out slowly, "I hope that you make it, and if you make it, I hope that someday you can come back."

"I hope so, too," she said. "Rick, I do plan on coming back," *if I make it*, she wanted to say. And she wanted to tell him about the plan her grandmother had, but she had promised not to tell

101

anyone. "Someday, Mr. Rivers is finally going to get in trouble. I just know it. It will all catch up to him. And then, maybe then I'll be safe. And I can come back, and just live my life, without having to worry. But for now, I just have to do this."

"She gave away her diamond necklace?" Rick almost sounded shocked when Alexandra finally told him what was in the box that she had earlier handed to Laura.

He drove his Pontiac directly behind the BMW and Alexandra sat in the passenger seat next to him. The traffic was light this time at night; the roadway almost empty. And no one seemed to be following them.

"Well, we originally were going to give away those old silver goblets that were put away in storage, but," she began, "then I found out why they had been locked away out of sight for so long." She explained the whole story. She did not like to talk about it. No one in the family did. It was a part of the family history that they would rather keep in the closet, the way their mother's first husband was killed, and what their mother did after that. "She found out we planned to give those away, and she wasn't happy about it, at all. But in the end, she felt sorry for her, so she decided to give the diamond necklace away to send with her. It's a kind gesture. And she has more than enough jewelry."

"She certainly does," he agreed. "More than enough . . . So, those old things belonged to your father? And they really are that ancient?"

"Yes, they really are that ancient. They came along with the silver dagger she keeps in her desk, the one she uses as a letter opener." She leaned back in the seat, enjoying the night wind as it ran through her hair.

"I still don't understand why she's taking this risk." Rick could not cease to worry for her. Laura had spent the day sleeping beside him, and had left holding back the tears. "She should stay and hide until this blows over."

"It's not going to go away, Rick," Alexandra said. "She has to do this. She's not just doing this to protect herself; she's doing it to protect us. And there's another reason," she continued, "another reason why she has to go."

"What's that?" He reached to turn off the radio. The signal was beginning to get weak and more static than music could be heard now. It was the original radio from when the car was built. "One of these days I've got to put a better radio in this car."

"From what she's told you, she was never allowed to do anything on her own; she was never allowed to learn to be independent by her controlling father. She didn't know how to handle her own money, or shop for groceries, or even drive. You taught her almost everything, Rick. You even had to show her how to do her own laundry. Remember?"

He remembered. It was almost sadly comical to find a grown woman who did not even know how to do laundry or cook for herself. "Yeah. So?"

"Do you think maybe, in a way, she's become dependent on you?"

"No. I taught her to take care of herself. How could you say that? She doesn't depend on me. I even taught her to use jumper cables, and how to change a tire." He had to talk her into learning to do that. "You could be thousands of miles away from the nearest garage," he warned. She finally agreed to learn how to do it. And she did it. She finally learned to change a tire, while in Italian designer heels and expensive satin Capri pants.

"I mean emotionally, Rick."

"Oh, now come on."

"Yes, really," she insisted. "Maybe, Rick, in a way, she needs to prove it to herself that she can really do things on her own." And she pointed ahead at the taillights of the BMW. "You see?

103

You said it yourself; she's been driving for probably less than a year. So what does she do? She doesn't get on a plane, she doesn't get on a bus, or a train. Instead she decides to drive across country. I'm actually amazed at this girl's courage and determination; even though I agree with you, that the smart thing to do would be to hide out somewhere."

He thought about it for a moment, and was silent, then said, "Maybe you're right. But I don't like it. I don't like the idea of losing someone I care about. Twice."

She knew he was talking about his wife. "But we outlive all of them, don't we? It just happens that way. It's sad, but it always happens that way, Rick. You have to know that, any time you get involved."

"I know," he said. "But why so soon? It's not fair." But he knew his sister was right. Laura had to do what she had to do. And that was that.

"How long do you think it will take her," she asked, to change the subject, "to get to the other side of the country?"

He hesitated and then said, "A long time ago I read an article in a car magazine." He began, thinking back and trying to remember. "These idiots decided to have a coast to coast race, starting from the east coast, and the finish line was in California. They lightened up their cars as much as possible, added extra fuel tanks, things like that. Some of the things they did weren't exactly safe. Some of them took drugs to stay awake; or they drove with a partner and would switch drivers, to keep running straight, all the way, non-stop. I think I remember now; the winner made it in something like slightly over thirty two hours. But she's going to stay within the speed limit, I hope." He quietly made some calculations. "I think it's about three thousand miles across the continent. If she stops just to eat and sleep, fill up on gas. I don't know . . . if she stays out of heavy traffic . . . maybe about a week."

"We should turn around now," she said. "It's three hours until dawn." And they had been following her for almost three hours. "No one is following her, except us."

"I know," he said, reluctantly, "I know, and I'll have to stop somewhere to buy gas again. This car eats like a pig. I'm glad they have all night gas stations these days." And so he pulled off the highway.

He wished he could follow her, all the way. But he knew he could not.

"Rick," she said. "She'll be back. I just know it. I don't know how I know, but I just feel it somehow. But right now, you have to let her go. She just has to do this."

Josephine sat at the kitchen table in her slightly drafty house studying late into the night. The rest of her family, not being nocturnal, not having inherited the DNA that forced them to live at night, had gone to sleep hours ago. She listened to the wind outside; and she could feel it seep through the windows, even though they were shut tightly. She was trying to manage working nights while taking classes part time at the community college, also at night. It wasn't easy but there was no other way she was going to get an education; unless she buried herself in debt from loans. Several open textbooks, purchased second hand and obviously used, were spread out on the table. She gazed at them through the haze of boredom, and wondered what kind of people specialized in writing such horrifyingly dull stuff.

She listened to the cold wind that came with early spring. It was the long sad cry of the death of winter, she imagined. Its almost never ending wail rushed through the trees outside, making a few branches tap against the glass pane of the window. She looked out through the window into the darkness suddenly when she heard a howl that cried out along with the wind. She wondered if it were a coyote off in the distance.

Or a wolf. She wasn't sure which, and she didn't really care.

Josie almost envied Sharona. She wondered how wonderful and amazing it must be to be able to wander through different worlds the way she did, to see things that almost no one else could see. Josephine just needed to get herself an education so she wouldn't need to stay in a dead-end job forever, or for a few centuries, at least. Sharona was doing almost the same thing; working, trying to figure out what she wanted to do with life, and in addition she could take the shape of a wolf and enter into the spirit realm. Way cool.

She then reflected on the other girl's situation and remembered that she had been homeless and on her own, sleeping in her car, existing at the cold edge of reality. And that she had lost almost everything. Not cool.

She took a sip from the luke-warm mug that was next to her, and decided to check her messages on her laptop. She reached across the table and pulled it close and opened it up. She then realized that she must have checked her messages about eight times tonight already, even though she wasn't expecting to receive any. She just stared into the bright screen out of sad boredom.

But now there was a message. It was another one from this person on the other side of the country, CoolLeon1, also known as Leon Ramirez Andreyev. She was curious what this was, because she had not gotten anything from him in a while. She read it, "We sent out the package, please let us know if it arrives safe." She typed back, "We will let you know as soon as it gets here."

Laura awakened into complete darkness and mild confusion. At first, she had no clear memory of where she was. Then she realized she was in a cheap motel that she found somewhere off the highway. Slowly, she recalled the events of the past few days, and finally remembered: she was on the road escaping from the man that her father had sent to kill her.

She had checked in yesterday during the late afternoon after becoming exhausted from driving for she did not know how long. She had checked in, came into her room, pulled the heavy draperies shut so no one could see her from outside, and then finally collapsed onto the stiff and uncomfortable bed into oblivion. She wasn't quite sure exactly where she was now, but realized it was most likely somewhere in Nevada. She didn't care, as long as she was waking up alive. For the hours she drove, she imagined she had gotten a good distance.

Laura opened her eyes and saw only darkness, but the darkness no longer frightened her as it did when she was a child. She had much more terrifying things to worry about. She was glad for the darkness; it meant no one could see her. And if they couldn't see her, then they certainly couldn't aim properly.

She listened and became aware that she could hear the couple in the next room arguing. Perhaps they had woken her up. She reached for a pillow to cover her head when their yelling got louder. Now they were screaming.

She thought of Rick, and his generally quiet demeanor, and wished he were with her, if not to protect her, then just for company and to listen to his offbeat commentary on everything and anything.

Thinking of him made her remember that he made her promise to check the car's oil each time she stopped. It was a long way to go, and she knew he was probably right. Check the oil, check the tires, and check the coolant. He reminded her of these things perhaps twenty times before she got on the road. "But it's a new car," she protested. "It should be fine."

"It's going to be a rough trip for any car," he said. "Hey, I know what I'm talking about," he said. "You don't get a car to last as long as mine has unless you take care of it."

The woman in the next room began to cry. The man roared at her to shut the fuck up. She heard a slap, then a shrill scream. She pulled the pillow tightly over her ears, but it did not help to block out the sound.

Laura wondered if she should walk over to the next room and knock on the door, or if she should call down to the front desk to complain. She dared not; it would draw attention to herself. She needed to avoid that if she was going to make it to the other side of the continent without being found and shot at again. The hit man had missed twice. He might not miss a third time.

"Damn it." She sat up and threw the pillow against the wall where the noise was coming from. "Shut up." But she knew they would not hear her.

She switched the light on and looked around the room. It was not a luxury hotel, such as the kind she had stayed in previously when she was known as Laura Rivers, heiress, daughter of the notorious billionaire Augustus Rivers. No, she realized, the place she was now staying was what Rick would refer to as a dump. The sheets smelled of something, something she could not quite identify. The mattress was lumpy. The bedspread was an unattractive burnt orange, as were the soft chairs and matching draperies. The carpet was a dark brown. She stared down at it and it disturbed her to realize what this particular shade of brown reminded her of. "These are your new surroundings, Laura Blasko," she said to herself. "Get used to it." The room did not have a chandelier hanging from the ceiling, or a balcony that looked down at a swimming pool.

No. It was a dump.

She thought of Rick again. He had saved her life. In a way, she realized he had saved her from her own miserable foolishness. He had taken in homeless kids to save them from the streets as well. He was so unlike her father. Rick the vampire, content to just exist every night, taking in homeless kids; while her father cared for nothing but himself and his cold money, his private jets, his collection of exotic cars, his stable of thoroughbred horses, and the multitude of corporations he controlled.

And she wondered what her life might now become if Zelda's plan did not work, and she could not return to where she now called home. She had a college degree, but it was earned in the name of Laura Rivers. Would she end up working as a cleaning lady in a cheap motel like this one? Would she end up waitressing, mopping floors, cleaning toilets?

The thought did not please her as she was used to living in comfort, even though her childhood was plagued with the misery of growing up with a cold father and an unpredictably frivolous stepmother for parents. She had no secretarial skills, or any other skills that could earn her a living. Back home, she was a grade school art teacher. But wherever she landed, she knew she couldn't just arrive and ask for the job of her choice. The sad realization dawned on her that she might have to clean toilets and mop floors one day.

But she tried to reassure herself. Zelda's plan would work. Augustus Rivers would soon be getting a visit from the FBI, or the SEC, or the IRS, or all three at the same time. Maybe even the EPA. Yes, she said to herself, he was probably also long overdue for a visit from the EPA.

She tried to imagine several government owned vehicles driving up the long driveway to his opulent mansion, with perhaps a helicopter or two in the air above. The cars would contain people from all these government agencies that were known to average citizens by all these important sounding big letters. Then he would spend some time in a federal prison, after finding to his shock that he couldn't buy his way out of trouble as easily as he usually did. And then she could return home to everything she loved and cared about.

The woman in the next room continued to cry. A police siren could be heard off in a distance; it was coming closer. Perhaps another person staying in the dump made the call.

Soon Laura heard knocking on the door to the next room. "Police. Open up." She was glad she wouldn't be staying long.

When Muriel returned home from an evening college class she saw the police car in her driveway. She wasn't sure if she should be worried or not. But then she recognized the car and realized it was Karl Stepanek's.

She opened the back door to find Sharona sitting at the kitchen table laughing hysterically—laughing so hard that her blonde curls were shaking and her eyes were watering—while Karl was standing there with an amused look on his face.

He turned to Muriel. "I just came by to inform Miss Thiessen that a certain individual most likely won't be bothering her or her coworkers from now on."

Sharona looked at Muriel, still laughing but trying to get a hold of herself. "Sorry about the cop being here. It's really nothing. Just some guy. You know, the guy that always bothers the waitresses."

"I don't think he'll be a problem anymore," Karl said, with a smile that Muriel realized was a slightly less than professional smirk. "I've known Gary for quite a while. He plows during the winter and does odd jobs during the summer. He lives in a few rooms above the garage where the plow trucks are kept. He didn't finish high school. I picked him up a few times for minor trouble. That's about all there is to Gary. He has limited social skills and can't get a girlfriend so he has to annoy to get any fun in life."

"I know Sergeant Stepanek," Muriel said, so Sharona would not worry about her coming home to find a policeman visiting. "He's been here before, for stuff like this. I had a jerk hanging around my place once, but that was different."

110

"Oh well," she said to herself. "I have a ghost in my house, a werewolf renting a room, and my neighbors are vampires."

"Having a police car parked in the driveway is probably not a big deal like it would be if this was a city, but it's a small town," she said as she watched as the Sergeant headed for the door. "I'd offer you a cup of tea, Karl, but—"

"Thanks, I have to be going anyway." He looked back to Sharona, and smiled again. "Muriel knows I'm one of the people in town that don't care for coffee or tea."

"What?" Sharona seemed confused and then surprised when the realization came to her.

"That's right. Well, nice to see you both. Let me know if there's any more problems, but I doubt it." He started on his way out.

"Oh my God," Sharona said. "Officer, I didn't know," she began laughing again as he walked out. "Is everyone in this town?"

Muriel dropped her heavy book bag down on the table and reached for the teakettle that was on the stove to fill it with water. "No, not everybody. I guess it's supposed to be a secret that a lot of people know but don't talk about, or they try to keep quiet about it, or something like that."

"Okay, well," she hesitated, then finally said it, "anyway, the pig came to the police station all upset about seeing a big scary wolf. But the Sarge has him convinced that it was probably just all in his head. I mean, I figure maybe you must know about that stuff too, because you know Josie? Right?"

"Yup, I know," Muriel said, rolling her eyes slightly. "I guess you never know what secrets you'll find in a small boring town like this one." And she reached up in the cabinet above the stove for the box of teabags. "Want one?"

"Sure. Thanks."

They heard the police car's engine start and then heard the car back out of the driveway.

"This little town isn't even on most maps," Muriel said. "Sometimes I think maybe that's why. They don't want to attract attention."

"You don't mind, do you?" Sharona asked, looking down at the dark and scratched wood of the old kitchen table.

"Mind what? That you can turn into a wolf?" The teakettle began to whistle.

"Well, I don't actually—"

"I know. Sophie explained it. She's very old, and she knows a lot. It's amazing the things she knows. She only told me because I asked. You came here with a wolf pelt in your bag, and then I saw a wolf run across the road. So I figured it out. But I had to ask her, because otherwise I thought I might be imagining things." She got two mugs and poured the hot water and sat down at the table. "Don't worry, Sharona. In this neighborhood, I'm sure you'll fit in just fine."

"How many are there?"

"What? Vampires? I don't know. Quite a few, I guess. I don't know all of them, just some of them. They've been around here a long time. How about you? Are there a lot of people like you?"

"I think I might be the last one," she said as she reached for the mug with both hands. It was still too hot to drink. She watched as the steam rose from the cup and waited for it to cool.

"They thought they were the last of their kind, too. But they're not. They found that out." She pulled a two inch thick book out of her bag. "This is so incredibly dull."

"What is it?"

"Calculus. I hate it. But I have to take it. I wish I could study the kinds of things I have discovered after moving to this town and have some kind of career that involved that sort of thing. A relative of mine did once, a long time ago. It would be way more interesting. But I can't. It has to be kept quiet. And we all know why."

"Yeah," she said sadly, "I know."

112

"Oh, and another thing," Muriel said. "Before I forget, a lady is coming to visit. She might only stay a little while. If she stays permanently, I'll have to charge her rent, because that would only be fair. She's coming from far away. She already knows that vampires exist, but she doesn't know anything about you. I mean, she doesn't know that werewolves exist. At least I don't think she does. It's kind of complicated. I guess it's a long story. But it's up to you what you want to tell her about yourself when you meet her."

Sharona sipped her tea and said, "Well, I guess I'll have to figure that out when she comes."

Rufus stared blankly at the textbook and once again his mind drifted off somewhere. It wasn't that the subject matter was difficult, but that is was horrifyingly dull. What would he ever need it for, anyway, he wondered. He still wasn't sure what he was going to do with the extremely long life that had been imposed upon him; not that he wanted to simply age and die by sixty-five or so, like almost everyone else. He had three hundred years to look forward to, and even if it wasn't going to be forever, it still seemed to be a pretty good deal. The only problem was that he had to drink blood. But what was he going to do with all that time? He stared at the blank white walls in the out of date kitchen while listening to the rhythm of the clock ticking, and wondered.

The private eye that was hired to find his father had no success, but Rick had reminded him more than once that the former police detective was no Sherlock. They had hired him because they knew him, and he was probably the only private investigator in town. Rick told him also that Detective Martin Atkinson lived in the same apartment building as his sister did, and that she lived one floor above, and it took years for Martin to stop being freaked out about living in the same building as a vampiress.

They never bothered to tell Martin that the building was owned by Rick's family.

Maybe that could be something to do? He could become a private investigator, and then find his father himself. He probably wouldn't need long division for that. He thought of what he would need to join the profession and remembered some detective movies he had seen. He would probably need a gun, maybe some spy equipment, and a cool car. Definitely he would need a cool car. Every TV detective had a cool car.

He thought of his family situation again and it came to him that he wasn't even sure if he could locate his mother to ask her questions about where his dad may have gone. He recalled that after he had been on the streets for a while he headed back to his home to see if the man who had been beating him up was still around, hoping to maybe come home again to stay. But when he arrived he found that the house was locked up and empty. He wandered the neighborhood and ran into a friend who told him that his mother finally kicked the man out, but then shortly after that she went somewhere—maybe to Mexico—with another man she had met online.

He almost felt as if Rick and the few other vampires he knew were the only family he had right now. And Miss Rivers—now Miss Blasko—but she had left a few nights ago, and no one was sure if she would be able to come back.

He wondered where Rick was. He had heard Rick's car come in to park behind the house. Usually Rick came in to check on him, to make sure he was studying or at least not doing anything that might make trouble. If Rick wasn't upstairs he was usually downstairs watching over the gallery, hoping a few customers would drift in to buy something. But it was late and the gallery had been closed for business hours ago. He could be in the back room behind the gallery where he worked on his paintings, but it seemed more quiet than usual down there.

Out of boredom he got up to go look for him. He needed an excuse for when he finally found him, because Rick would ask him why he wasn't studying. He would ask Rick something foolish, like where did you get such a cool car, or how much would you have to save before you could get one like it. Or he might announce what he planned to do with his life, and then maybe ask how he could get a cool car so he could become a private eye.

He drifted down into the gallery and found that it was in darkness.

There was a slight glow of soft light coming from the back room where Rick usually worked. Rick felt comfortable working in dim light, he realized. And now Rufus could perceive the chemical odor of the paints. He was beginning to realize that he had a better sense of smell than most people did, as he could distinguish the scent from the next room as he made his way through the semidarkness.

He walked through the dark gallery and headed toward the room in the back where various works in progress were kept until finished and ready for display and sale, and saw Rick in the soft and slightly dim light with his back to him, working at his easel.

"Hey, Rick."

"What?" he snapped, as if he didn't want to be bothered.

Rufus went ahead anyway, "Guess what?"

Rick didn't answer, and so the boy came up beside him . . . and saw a tear drift slowly down Rick's pale cheek.

"What do you want now, kid?"

"You okay?" Rufus asked.

"Yeah, fine. The paint is making my eyes water, that's all." Rick wiped the moisture away with his sleeve. "I'm working. I have to keep the bills paid, you know. Weren't you supposed to be trying to figure out this thing called math?"

"Ah . . . yeah, okay." Rufus understood. "Yeah, never mind. It was nothing. Yeah, I know. I still gotta study that boring crap."

Rufus turned to go back upstairs, but he knew what it was about. Rick missed her, or he was worried about her. Maybe Rick worried that she might not return, not ever. Or he worried that she would meet someone else while she was away. Or a combination of all of those at once.

Rufus wasn't sure if he had ever seen two people in love before. His mother had a series of what she referred to as "relationships." The relationships sometimes paid the bills. Sometimes the relationships beat her; sometimes the relationships beat Rufus. Often the relationships beat both Rufus and his mother at the same time. Sometimes the relationships brought drugs into the house. There were times when the relationships made his mother happy, but more often they made her cry.

He had left home because of one of his mother's relationships. He now realized that none of the relationships were anything that could be considered love. They were simple dependency for money, or drugs, or both, or just simple neediness. None of them were love.

He wondered if the difference between the types of relationship his mother would often get involved with, and real love, was that maybe the relationship hurt when that person was in your life, but love hurt when that person was gone.

He went back to the kitchen and tried to focus on the book again.

She twitched as she suddenly became aware that her back hurt from sitting for she did not know how long. Previously she had been only aware of the endless dark solid ribbon of cars ahead of her on the never-ending and unmoving highway.

She reached to shut off the radio, because it was only background noise and she was sick of hearing it. It seemed like everyone with the ability to call into the radio station had the solution to each and every political and social problem that existed in the country. "And I'll tell you what to do with those people," the anonymous voice from over the airwaves announced. "You just round up all those people, and then you line them all up—" And finally it was turned off.

Next she hit the button to open up the driver side window and smelled the dull stench of exhaust and stale city air. Ahead of her, the little boy in the back of the dark gray SUV bounced up and down and made faces at her. He looked at her and stuck his tongue out. His parents seemed unaware of his behavior as his father tossed food wrappers and soft drink cans out of the SUV and onto the pavement. She continued to ignore the boy as he started giving her the finger with both of his little hands.

She looked away and grabbed the coffee she had purchased probably over two hundred miles ago and realized it was nearly empty and what little was left was cold. People all around blasted their horns at each other's cars. Someone down the road several cars away shouted at someone else to "Freakin' move it!"

But nothing was moving. Laura was experiencing her first real traffic jam.

The cars moved along slowly, inch by inch it seemed, for miles, for hours, endlessly. She wondered if she might get to her destination faster if she could get out and walk. She leaned her head on the leather wrapped steering wheel and swore.

Finally, after probably another long hour, the cars began to move along again, like a vast herd of animals suddenly set free. They moved cautiously at first, then slowly and steadily. As her BMW got closer to where the problem on the road was, she saw the scene of an accident, and realized that the traffic had come to a standstill because everyone else had to slow down to look at the automotive carnage of twisted and crushed metal, fallen auto parts, and broken glass scattered across the road. And then she noticed the blood splattered on the pavement . . . and the beer cans.

Somewhere up ahead the ambulance was speeding along ahead of the traffic. Off in the distance she could hear the siren.

Sharona and Josephine walked out of work together and headed for their cars. Their long shift was over, and they were both tired. Josie told Sharona that she couldn't wait to get out of her uniform; it had coffee spilled all over it from when a tray on the countertop overturned. Sharona told Josie that her feet hurt from a long night of waiting tables and then helping to clean up after the restaurant closed. It was a hard night, but they got paid, plus some decent extra money in tips. Sharona planned to use some of her money from tips to buy herself some things at the thrift store that was near the center of the small town. Most of her clothes had been destroyed in the house fire that she had escaped from.

Behind them one of the other waitresses who was walking out of the truck stop yelled, "Hey, wait for us!"

And another girl who was leaving laughed and called out after them, "Yeah, don't go out there alone, there's wolves in the parking lot!"

They slowed down and waited for the other two to catch up. They knew they had to humor them and pretend they didn't know where the wolf really came from. They didn't leave the parking lot until everyone else's car was started and in motion.

Sharona watched as Josie's car drifted out of the dark parking lot. She was tired but it was a nice, clear night. She didn't have to get up early in the morning so she could sleep late. She decided that she wanted to go out. She could wander the night wherever she wanted to go, and her feet wouldn't hurt then. There was no pain on the other side.

The she wolf looked on as the old Indian sat before his eternal campfire deep in the darkest part of the ancient forest, where few if any white men had ever cared to tread. The old one sat and gazed sadly into the ghostly flame that only burned brightly in the spirit realm and could not be seen by most of the living. She listened as he talked on in his own language. He talked perhaps to himself, or to the forest, or he talked to other spirits long since passed on.

Then suddenly he looked up and said, "I see you, Spirit Wolf."

Still, the wolf was motionless.

"You have come back. I see you there beyond the trees. My people knew of the shapeshifters before the white man came and took everything away, took away our land, took our way of life. Everything is gone now. Only I, Gray Eagle, remain to watch over the forest. I think these trees above might be the last trees in the world, Spirit Wolf. This lake beyond the forest might be the last lake. The meadow on the other side of the lake might be the last meadow. The birds in the air and the animals that live here might be the last birds and animals. The white man came long ago and he cut down everything, first with axes, then with machines. The world is being eaten by the white man's machines. Where will all the animals go? Where will the birds go? I think maybe outside of this forest there is nothing, maybe only barren desert where there is no forest left. I do not know for sure. Maybe you know. Maybe you see more of the world where you travel. But when all the trees are gone, when all the animals and birds are dead, and when all the lakes are dried up, what will be left? I do not know." He reached to put small twigs onto the fire. "One day, finally, when all the land is dead, and nothing will grow, the white man will have to learn that he cannot eat his dollars that he got from cutting down all the forests."

The wolf came closer to the campfire and sat facing Gray Eagle and he continued to talk, "This I do know, because I hear other spirit voices that are carried in the night wind. Someone comes from afar, and evil follows." He pulled a twig out of the fire and pointed the flaming end at her. "Evil will come soon, Spirit Wolf. Be awake when it comes."

Sharona awoke with a start. She ran her hand down the fur of the gray wolf pelt to remind herself she had not been dreaming. She sat up and looked out the window; it was early morning, the stars just beginning to fade.

The old Indian sent her back with his mysterious warning. She lay her head back down on the pillow and wondered what it all could mean. Could what he said be some sort of dire portent, or just the rambling of a sad and long dead protector of the forest? She decided to try and get some sleep, and try to figure it out later. It would soon be daylight, and so there was no one she could ask; no one that was knowledgeable enough to help her figure out what it could be about.

What did Gray Eagle mean, "Evil will come soon?"

Augustus James Rivers the Third sat behind the huge and ornate antique mahogany desk that dominated the space he used as an office in his mansion, and he was very annoyed. The late morning sun glared through the windows, making the computer screen difficult to read. And in addition to that, the politician that he had handsomely paid to get things done for him did not deliver. As if any politician would ever keep a promise he made. But this one he had paid very well, and he expected something of value in return. Then there was the patch of dry and useless land he wanted to extract resources from, but these ridiculous anti-fracking people were at it again. They were complaining that "People lived near there." It was "Unsafe for the environment." And it could "Pollute the drinking water." Along with the endless and pathetic cry of "What about the children?" Those people who were foolish enough to live there needed to be removed somehow, and soon. He would have to think about that one.

Maybe a truck carrying hazardous chemical waste would crash nearby and they would have to be evacuated. Or, he thought, with a smirk on his face, maybe it would be easier not to evacuate the people. Maybe the people would conveniently all die when the truck carrying dangerous chemicals crashed. Then the waste could be cleaned up, but only just slightly, so people would be able to work nearby, but not live there—no, people would never be able to live there again—and then he could just buy the useless land cheaply.

He silently congratulated himself. Once again he had a brilliant solution that would get useless people out of the way, and be profitable.

The phone on his desk rang. Not many people had his private phone number. Maybe another job he had contracted out had been completed? His mood suddenly lifted with the hope that another small annoyance in his life would be gotten rid of. He answered it and listened, and then he suddenly barked, "What the hell do you mean she didn't go the airport? What? She's headed down the highway? Who taught the stupid little bitch how to drive a car?"

He leaned back in the large black Italian leather chair and continued to listen to the weak excuses. "Now look, Vito, you've taken care of these things before. This one should be easy. She's just a stupid girl. And you missed her twice? Damn it!" He swore. *Twice?*

What was the world coming to, when you couldn't just have a girl taken out so you could go on and think about things that were more important? He had to get rid of her. He had to. She was supposed to be dead. *Dead!* If she were found out there, somewhere, still alive, it wouldn't look good. He had her obituary printed in every major newspaper when she disappeared.

If she were still alive, it would make him appear to be dishonest. And that could be bad for business.

The man on the other end of the line continued to mumble, whine, and then finally reassure. Mr. Rivers stared up at the ceiling and exhaled slowly as he listened. Even the best in professional hired killers were stupid these days, he now realized. It made him sad. And the politicians he paid to get things done for him weren't much better. It was so hard to find good help. The world was lucky to at least have a few intelligent men like himself in it to run things and get things done efficiently.

He continued to listen and decided to finish up the conversation, "Okay, well at least you know where she's going. Why don't you just wait until she stops, and then do the job? I'm just curious where she'll land herself this time, so I can see what sort of riffraff she's associating herself with now. And when you do finally get around to it, Vito, don't miss! I pay you well enough not to miss. You've done plenty of jobs like this before. I don't know why taking out one stupid useless girl should be so difficult!" He slammed the phone down. "Damn it!"

He had bigger things to worry about than getting rid of the little bastard that came from his gold-digger first wife. When he thought about his first wife, it almost made him feel sick. She had been a fashion model. He had seen her in a magazine, and decided he would marry her. He gave her a good life, jewels, furs, everything. The least he could expect was loyalty. She had become just another problem he needed to have taken care of, along with her lover.

Somewhere down the hallway, he heard the old cleaning lady vacuuming, but he wasn't worried. He wondered how the hell long the foolish old bat had been in this country, but still she could not speak a word of English?

Oh well, he said to himself. Not everyone is smart enough to learn much beyond simple things. She had worked around the house for years and he still didn't know what the hell country she was from, but he didn't care. She dusted the furniture, she emptied the wastebaskets, she vacuumed the carpets, and she didn't know enough English to understand anything she might have overheard. So, he reasoned, that fact probably made her his most valuable employee. Hell, she might actually be smarter than the hit man he just got off the phone with.

He leaned back in the soft leather chair and gazed placidly out the window. He reassured himself that things would fall rightly into place, and get taken care of, one way or the other. He knew he always got his way, eventually. It was only a matter of time. If one politician didn't do the job, he would just pay another one to do it. That's all. He would get the land he wanted, and the people who were in the way would be gotten rid of. Just like Laura, they would all be gotten rid of. And if the hit man failed again, he would just have him taken care of, too.

He had other names in his Rolodex.

He thought a moment, and then came to the realization that this fool that he had sent chasing after Laura would need to be taken out soon, too, anyway. After doing so many jobs, he now knew way too much.

What was that other person's name? He tried to remember . . . Brice something. He decided that when this job was finished, he would give this Brice person a call.

Mr. Rivers then briefly looked at his computer and gently tapped the keyboard to get to the right screen. It revealed a satellite image, a road map as viewed from the sky. What on earth was she doing there? He wondered. Where was she going? He didn't really care, and it didn't matter. Most likely she had gotten some foolish idea into her simple little head that drove her on. It would be taken care of when she finally stopped running, or arrived at wherever she was headed.

He smiled as he looked out at the sunny, bright and pleasant morning. Yes, he said to himself, things would eventually work out for the best.

They always did.

Laura's car glided along the rural highway at effortless speed. She leaned back in the leather seat and stretched her leg out as it met the accelerator. Finally, her back had stopped hurting after a long night's sleep in a quiet little motel called the Old Country Inn. It was a good name for it, since it was out in the country, literally in the middle of nowhere. Laura had stopped last night just after dusk, filled the gas tank, and had a decent meal along with a few drinks to make her almost forget the reason for her long journey. But that was hundreds of miles behind her.

Now the sun blazed gently through the windshield and she was glad for its warmth. Both windows open, the cool wind rushed through her hair and caressed her face. It seemed like several days since she had felt the fresh air or the sun's light, for she had begun her escape in dark of night and in the first few days saw only sad gray skies above. She looked ahead now and saw endless fields of green rushing by as the BMW sped down the road; endless fields of green interrupted by the occasional small group of dairy cows, horses, small farms, and modest homes with old cars or trucks in front of them. And then after passing a small cluster of homes surrounding a town with a few buildings and a simple church, she drove through another endless plane of nothing but tall grass.

She thought of Rick and felt sad that he missed out on seeing beautiful days like this. She decided that when she returned she would attempt to sketch a scene from memory and give it to him, or maybe she would attempt it once she finally stopped and came to her destination. She always brought her sketchpad wherever she went. Laura so wished he could have come with her; no, she wished she didn't have to leave at all. But she wasn't safe, and her being there made others around her unsafe.

And now she realized, if she had remained, she wouldn't have any opportunity to see what she was seeing now. She had never seen such vast beautiful and natural emptiness before. It reminded her of rural landscape paintings that were admired in museums, only what she saw before her was real. And for a brief moment, she wondered if the pioneers of long ago had driven their covered wagons over the very same lands she was speeding across.

Laura was travelling alone down a lonely highway and she was seeing America. Not the America that most people who travelled across the continent wanted to see. Not the Grand Canyon, not Mount Rushmore, not the majestic national parks. She was seeing cheap motels and quiet country inns, traffic jams and rural landscapes, concrete cities and beautiful farmland; and she knew now that the man standing at an exit ramp with a sign saying he "Will Work for Food" was living in the same America as those who lived in the mansions of Beverly Hills.

For all that she saw before her, whether beautiful or tragic, was in the same vastness of the American continent. It was real, and seemed endless.

Rufus returned from the nightclub where Leon had given him a part time job helping to clean up after closing, sweeping floors, wiping down tables, and bringing the trash out to the back alley near the delivery entrance. It was his first real job, his first legal job, that is. He had done other things before to earn money, when he was living on the streets. That was the type of work he would rather forget about. He was glad for the new job. The pay was okay, and Leon was good to work for. It

125

wasn't a cool job, or a private eye job, but it was probably the first time he worked for someone who was not going to try to exploit him.

And now he returned to Rick's place and intended to try and study before falling asleep at dawn. He came up the stairs and saw Rick in the same place he had been for the past several nights. He was standing there in the living room that was on the upper floor, gazing silently out the front window, ceramic mug in hand, looking out and far away into the night, staring down at the dark street, his eyes directed toward where the main road met the exit ramp that led up to the highway.

Rufus sat at the kitchen table; his books were already there, but he didn't open any of them. "Heard anything yet?" he asked.

"Hmm?" Rick turned and looked at him. "No. No, we haven't heard anything yet. But she won't call or make any contact until she gets there, just in case the phones were bugged."

"You think her dad would do that?"

Rick stared out the window again. "He's not her real father, Rufus; and I don't know if he would do that. Maybe the man Mr. Rivers hired would do that. Can't be too careful. The bastard shot out the front window in my gallery. We're lucky there weren't any customers down there when it happened. That was the second time he tried to kill her, or maybe the third." He remembered what Laura had told him about Mr. Rivers ordering a riding instructor to put her on an unruly horse. "I don't know. It's been awhile. It's hard to guess where she is right now. It would depend on how fast she's driving, how often she stops to rest; things like that." He considered telling him about the coast to coast race he had read about once, but decided it most likely would just bore the kid. "A run like that can be made in something like 32 hours, by driving nonstop and very fast. It's been done before. But she'll drive at a normal rate of speed, and stop to sleep along the way."

126

"You're worried about her, huh?"

"She's out there, somewhere, if she's still alive. If the man her father . . . If the man Mr. Rivers hired has gotten to her, we probably won't know about it, not for a while. I just want her to be safe, that's all."

Laura stood outside of her car and looked back down the long road. It was semi-dark, and lightening streaked across the gray sky. The air seemed filled with a light mist of fog, but yet did not feel damp or cold. She turned to look ahead and then she saw the wolf. She didn't understand why she wasn't afraid that there was a wolf standing there in the middle of the road, like she should have been.

Instead of being afraid, Laura simply stood there, looking alternately down the road at the direction she had come from; and then back at the wolf, which stood in the middle of the road that she was going to be continuing on to get to her destination. She knew that she needed to continue her journey as soon as she figured out why she wasn't in her car, and why she was standing there passively with a wolf so close by.

Lightening shot across the night sky again, but there was no sound of thunder to answer it. She turned and glared down the road, staring past where her car was parked, as if she was expecting something, or someone, to come this way.

"Who's following you?"

She whirled around when she heard a soft feminine voice, and saw the wolf was no longer there. Instead there was a girl, probably no older than sixteen, with worn and faded jeans, a long sleeved gray cotton shirt, and . . . what was that on her head? It was the head of a wolf, or the part of a wolf pelt where the head would be, covering the girl's hair, with the dark gray ears sticking up. The rest of the thick furred gray pelt ran all the way down the girl's back, the black tail touching the pavement.

She couldn't quite make out the girl's face; it was too dark to see, like twilight.

"Who's following you?" the girl quietly asked again. "And why is he following you?"

"Is someone following me?" It was the only answer Laura could give, and then. "Who are you? Wasn't there a wolf there? I'm sorry. I think I'm a little confused here. I really don't know what's going on right now. Where is this place? Am I lost? I'm trying to head northeast. I think I'm lost. I didn't think anyone was following me. I really didn't. I think I saw a wolf. Should we be worried? About the wolf, I mean?"

"Go back to sleep," the girl said. "You're just dreaming. That's all."

"I don't know what the old Indian could have meant, either, dear," Sophie said.

It was late in the day when Sharona went wandering through the thrift store that was near Annasophia's dress shop. She bought herself a pair of almost new leather flat heeled brown boots, a pair of not too badly faded jeans, and a denim jacket that was in decent condition, along with a few other things. It was dusk when she left to go out to her car but then she looked across the street and saw a light on in the dress shop.

"Tammy wanted to leave early," Sophie explained. "She hasn't been feeling well. It's her arthritis, I think. I had to come in a little earlier than usual because some ladies might come by to try on their gowns and make sure they all fit right before taking them. Tammy is the lady works here during the day, you know," she continued, leaning over the counter where the cash register was. She sighed, "She might retire in a few years; I'll have to find a replacement some day. But I hope it's not too soon. Maybe if you're still around by then, maybe I'll teach you to run the shop? Would you like that?"

128

"Maybe," Sharona said with some enthusiasm. "Yeah, I'd have to see what I'm doing then, though. But I'd like to." She then sat down in a chair that was by the entrance, "Sorry to barge in like this. I just thought I should tell you what Gray Eagle said. Oh, yeah, I figured out his name. In English, I guess his name means Gray Eagle. Anyway, he said someone comes from far away, and evil follows. So I got worried, and I don't know if it's right to do this, but," she hesitated, "I sort of tried to communicate with her, the lady who's coming here from far away. I mean, in her dreams, while she slept."

Sophie gazed down at Sharona. "I have lived a long time and I am not usually impressed by most things. But, Sharona . . . well, never mind. What did she say?"

"She didn't seem to know what was following her, either. It's not her that's evil; I know that. She's innocent. I can just tell. Something, or someone, seems to be coming down the road in the same direction, far behind, but coming. I didn't see who, or what, so, . . . I just don't know. I don't think Gray Eagle knows either. It's hard to explain. It's like when you feel bad weather coming, or something. The wind shifts, or the temperature suddenly drops, you see dark clouds all of a sudden, and you know there will be bad weather. Well, over there, it's like you kind of sense when something really bad is coming. It's not like you see it or hear it, you just sort of feel it. I don't know how to explain it, really. And I don't know what to do, because I really don't know what it is, or who it is, the evil that's following her. I think it's still far away now, but it might arrive here eventually. I really don't know, because," she admitted, "I'm still a little new at this."

"Do you think you should tell Karl?"

Sharona looked confused.

"The policeman. I just call him Karl."

"Oh. I don't know. Do you want me to?"

"I'll tell him for you," Sophie said, and she looked at her watch. "They were supposed to be here for that wedding dress that is in the front window, and the bridesmaid gowns. I called them and told them when I could come and open up for them. They should have been here by now. Young people today, they just don't seem to think that keeping appointments is important anymore."

Sharona looked around and saw the five satin pink gowns hanging on a rack in the back of the shop, ready to be picked up. They were beautiful, and she couldn't imagine them being abandoned there for very long. She noticed the rest of the shop was quite small, probably smaller than Sophie's living room, but that there was a room in the back with sewing machines and bolts of fabric stacked on shelves. The rug in the main area looked hand braided, but worn from many years. An ornate handmade quilt hung from the wall, and she imagined it might be expensive; if the gowns were costly, then the quilt would be worth more with all the work that had gone into creating it. In the corner, a small space heater glowed, for which she was grateful.

"You were right to come and tell me," Sophie said quietly. "We thank you, Sharona. We will be looking out now, for whatever it is that this Gray Eagle you talk to predicts is coming."

"I hope he's wrong," Sharona shrugged. "You know, sometimes spirits just say crazy things." But she knew she had felt it also. "And I hope I'm wrong, too."

The phone rang, and Sophie answered it, "Sophie's Dress Shop. Hello? Oh. Yes? Yes, of course I'll stay open and wait for you. Thank you for calling." And she hung up. "The girls are out having a few drinks before picking up their gowns. Good grief. Well, at least they called. I have things at home I could be working on." She sighed and looked up toward the ceiling, then suddenly asked, "Well, have you heard from Ben?"

130

She hesitated and then said, "No, Sophie, I'm sorry. He's been quiet lately. I don't know why. I saw him once and he talked and talked, but now . . . Sometimes ghosts are like that, I guess. They manifest and then go quiet for a while. I'll try and reach out to him for you."

It was late in the morning and Laura held onto the large coffee that she got from a fast food place with one hand and she held the steering wheel with the other. She took a sip and then finally noticed the coffee was starting to get lukewarm even though it was still half full. She put it back in the cup holder, and now that the road was nearly empty with less traffic, she relaxed and began to wonder again about the strange dream she had the other night.

What did it all mean? Did it mean that someone was following her? Or did it just mean that she worried about someone following her? How could anyone be following her, since she took off in dark of night and spent the first few days looking in the review mirror half the time? She felt quite sure no one was following behind her, and hoped that she was right.

And why was there a wolf in her dream? And then there was a strange girl with a wolf pelt over her head, with ears sticking up and fluffy tail dragging along the ground? What was that all about? Was it something bad that she had eaten before falling to sleep? She decided to try and put it out of her mind and try to forget.

She looked ahead through her windshield and saw snow flurries begin to blow by in the cold wind. She had never driven in snow before, and also believed it was too late in the year for snow. But then, she realized, it probably meant she was getting closer to her destination, because it would probably still be cold where she was going. Above the sky was gray, like the road under the car. The snow did not cling to the pavement or remain on the ground. It seemed instead to continually blow around in the air, the small delicate white flurries never landing anywhere.

It was like the toy snow globe she remembered that her grandfather had given her when she was a little girl. She remembered how the snow globe was one of the few things that brought a small amount of happiness into her childhood, and how she would stare into it endlessly, imagining the snow was real, and imagine that she was dancing in it, dancing wild and free in the middle of a snow filled fairy tale forest.

After a while the snow became thick, making it harder to see. She put the windshield wipers on, and then the defroster. Then up ahead, she saw it: a woman and child standing by the road next to a broken down car. When she got close enough, she saw the desolate look on the woman's face and knew she had to stop. She simply could not go on and leave them stranded on the road and continue to drive on. She pulled the BMW over to the side of the road and in front of the other car. She got out and saw that the old Toyota had a flat tire.

"I was hoping someone would come by," the woman said, and then, "I don't got no phone. I can't afford no phone. If I had a phone, I couldn't call my husband anyway. We don't know where he is right now." She wore only a sweatshirt, jeans with holes in them, and worn out sneakers—not enough to fight the cold. Her dirty blonde hair was getting covered with snow. "I think he's gone to New Jersey with his new girlfriend."

The little girl stood shivering in the wind and said nothing.

"Well," Laura began, "a friend of mine made me learn how to change a tire, and so—"

"You know how to change a tire?" The woman sounded as if she didn't believe it. "You do? Really?"

"Yes. I only did it once, though. Well, let's get the spare tire out, and see if we can get your car back on the road, okay?"

"You must be rich," the little girl with messy brown hair suddenly said, looking at the BMW. "You got a rich car."

Laura thought about how to respond. "If I was rich, I don't think I'd need to learn to change a flat tire. My chauffeur would do it for me," and she said it with a sad smile, remembering the days when she did have a chauffeur to take her wherever she wanted to go. But the chauffeur worked for her father, and so her life was restricted and tightly controlled.

"Well, the way he showed me was, you have to loosen the lug nuts a little bit first, before jacking the car up. Then after they're a little loose, you jack up the car, and get the wheel off." She thought about it out loud, trying to remember the process. "And, oh, let's get the spare and jack and things out first."

Laura used the small hydraulic jack that Rick had bought for her when she finally agreed to let him show her how to change a flat. He told her it would be easier to use than the cheap jacks the car manufacturers put in with the spare tires. He also gave her a long steel lug wrench that he said would be "easier for someone with small hands." When she looked closely at the tire, she noticed the tread was worn to almost nothing. Another thing she remembered Rick telling her was that it was important for the tread to be in good condition, or the tire would be dangerous. She imagined that if this tire is no good, then the rest would probably be unsafe also.

Lifting the heavy wheel was difficult, and so the two women managed to mount the spare onto the car together. Finally when the small spare tire was on, Laura spun the cross-shaped lug wrench to quickly tighten the lug nuts. She lowered the car back down to the pavement, and then she tightened the lug nuts a little more. When she was finally finished, she realized how cold she was.

"Oh, my God, I'm so glad you came," the woman said to Laura, hugging her. "I was praying someone would come. You must be an angel. I believe in angels, you know! I prayed for an angel, and you came. Except I was expecting it would be a strong, handsome guy!"

"Well," Laura wasn't sure if the woman seriously believed she was an angel or not, and she didn't know what else to say, "I guess now you know how to change a tire, too. And it's really cold out here." She looked at her delicate hands and saw they were now covered in filth and almost painful from the cold. She put her hands in the pockets of her hooded sweatshirt to warm them. She looked down and saw that that her blue jeans were also stained from kneeling on the pavement.

"Mommy, I gotta go the bathroom. Real bad," the little girl said. "Like, now."

Laura looked at her hands again and realized a washroom might be a good idea. "Is there a place nearby, off the highway, with a clean ladies room? Maybe a coffee shop?"

"Sure there is," the mother said. "Right off the next exit. Follow me."

Laura stared down at her untouched blueberry muffin and held onto the large coffee mug tightly, hoping its warmth would finally defrost her hands. She had just come back out of the ladies room where she had washed her hands the best she could, but the water was cold and the soap was the cheap kind that make her skin feel raw. And so her delicate hands still felt like ice.

At least the mother and little girl seemed happy. The girl, whose name she had learned was Christa-Belle—or something that sounded like it—was enjoying a chocolate donut and a large milk shake. And the mother, whose name she now knew was Linda, was also enjoying a frosted donut along with her own very large coffee.

In conversation Laura learned that Linda worked nights cleaning office buildings, vacuuming the carpets, cleaning the bathrooms, and emptying wastebaskets; she also worked weekends cleaning people's homes. And once again, Linda went on about not knowing where Christa-Belle's father had gone.

Linda listened patiently as Laura explained about her strange dream, ". . . and well, I took psychology in college and I keep wondering about it, and still, I have no idea what it could all mean. I almost never have strange dreams like that. That's what I was thinking about and wondering about when I saw your car. It was all so bizarre. Something about it seemed real, but then I woke up. In fact, the girl in the dream told me I was just dreaming. I just don't know why I would dream about seeing a wolf in the middle of the road. I don't know why I'm even telling you this, Linda. Maybe because you said you believe in angels. I just don't know what it could mean."

Linda was silent a moment and then said, "The wolf was real important to the Native American Indians. Maybe it was a spirit guide?"

"Spirit guide?"

"Yeah," said Linda, "you know, like a guardian angel that's an animal."

"Well, I really don't know. I never heard of such things."

"You said you were driving across country," Linda continued. "Maybe you'll find out what it all means when you get to where you're going?"

"I hope so. But maybe it was just a silly dream," Laura said, finally starting on her muffin.

They sat and talked for a while and finished their coffee and then Linda thanked her once again for helping to change her flat tire. "I gotta go to the ladies room myself." And she stood up.

Laura watched her until she went into the ladies room and then reached into her purse. She was nearly at her destination, and her cash was still holding out well enough. "Christa-Belle," she handed the little girl five one hundred dollar bills, "tell your mom to get all new tires for her car. And the rest she can use for groceries, or whatever she needs. Okay?" She got up and made her way back to the parking lot to her BMW, glad that she had

135

been able to help the woman and her little girl. She now realized that the road was teaching her more about real life, and that real life was more about helping others than it was about collecting designer purses.

She was close to the end of her journey. She might even make it by nightfall.

When Laura finally arrived at the place she had been instructed to go to, a wave of exhaustion began to overtake her. She wondered why she was told to arrive at this place, rather than to go directly to a person's home, or to go to the nearest motel and wait there. She dragged herself slowly through the glass double door and shuffled slowly in. The place was filled with people eating late night dinners, having a beer, talking, laughing, or having their second piece of pie.

She was ushered to a seat at a booth and handed a menu, but wondered if she was too tired to eat. She blinked, trying to stay awake.

Finally a waitress came over. "Hi!" she said, sounding awake and bright and cheerful. "What can we get yah?"

"I think I'll start with a coffee. Does someone named Josephine work here?"

"You must be Josie's cousin from out of town. She said you were coming to visit."

"Oh," she hesitated, but then even in the fog of her exhaustion she realized the story about her being a relative was a good cover, and so she decided to play along. "Yes. That's right. I'm coming to visit."

Her coffee was quietly delivered to her and she sipped it slowly and sleepily, not even noticing whether it was hot or cold or somewhere in between, or whether it was better or worse than all the other coffee that had kept her awake for her journey across the nation. She stared straight ahead, looking at various people, yet only seeing them as if in a dreamlike state.

Then suddenly, "Laura?"

She turned and looked up. The girl was pretty; a slender figure with jet black, glossy hair, skin fair as winter's first snow.

And that's how Laura knew who she was. She had that look about her. The same look that Rick and others of his kind had: that healthy, yet never in the sun look, and with a certain luminous quality in the eyes. She looked young, but Laura would not attempt to guess her age. For a brief moment, she imagined that maybe she was dreaming, and that she was safe and back home where she should be, with Rick and all his people, and that this lady was just another vampire that she had never met before.

Then the reality of it pierced her heart; she missed him. She wanted to get back into her car and drive back the way she came. But she was here. And she couldn't. To go back could mean death, for herself and for others she cared about.

"Hi," Laura said quietly. "You must be—"

"Josephine. Call me Josie." Then she said, "You look awfully tired."

Laura smiled weakly. "Yes . . . yes, I am. I'm awfully tired."

"Did you really, actually drive all the way from—?"

"Yes."

"I hope you stopped to rest along the way?"

"Oh, yes. I stayed in many places. But right now, I think I'm too exhausted to remember any of them."

"Okay, look," Josie said. "Finish your coffee. I'll make a few phone calls. We'll arrange for you to stay somewhere for the night. Tomorrow night, when you're a little more awake—"

"Thank you," she said, relieved at the thought of getting some sleep. Then she remembered, "And I have something I'm supposed to give to someone."

"I'm sure tomorrow night will be fine." She smiled briefly. "You made it here safely, that's what matters. We've arranged

137

for a place for you to stay where you'll be comfortable. I just need to make a phone call, and let them know you're here."

"Thank you," she yawned.

Rufus leaned back in the old and slightly uncomfortable wooden chair and looked around in the semi-darkness and listened to the near silence. He noticed that Rick hadn't talked much in past several nights, not since the time he complained that the vapors from the paints were "irritating his eyes." They were down in the lower level under the nightclub, along with Rick's older brother, the three of them sitting in silence, sipping from heavy lead crystal glasses while people danced to the music on the floor above their heads. The music echoed from above and at times it seemed the walls were vibrating.

Rufus worried about Rick but knew to leave him alone. He wished Rick would talk to him more, and tell him more details about what to expect from the next three hundred or so years of his potentially boring nocturnal life. That was another reason he hoped that Rick's girlfriend would be okay and come back in one piece. It wasn't that he didn't care about Laura himself; he did like her. She was very kind to help him with his homework, and he knew that very few people would even speak to a former homeless street kid—especially a kid that did what he did to be able to eat.

He looked around and saw that Rick looked down at the wooden table, as if gazing at nothing. Alex stared at Rick, and Rufus wondered if Alex might be worried about him also.

At another table some women sat together and talked quietly, almost whispering. One of them looked in their direction, and he wondered if they were talking about the situation. Vampires, he realized, probably gossip as much as most other people, especially since they all knew each other in this town.

He heard footsteps coming down the stairs, coming down from the floor above. He looked up and saw that it was Leon. He was not a vampire, but he was treated like one of the family since he was sort of adopted. He didn't know much about Leon, but Leon seemed to know every vampire in town, along with knowing everyone's personal business. He carried a small computer with him on his way down.

"Hey!" Leon called out. "You guys. She made it."

Rick looked up. "What?"

"She made it. She's okay."

He came to their table and pulled out a chair and sat down. "Look," he showed Rick the message on screen, "it's from Josie. She says she made it. They took her to stay at a friend's house. She's exhausted, but she's okay."

Rick pulled the computer closer so he could read it, then pushed it away. "Well, she's okay, then."

"What's up?" Leon said. "You should be happy."

"She'll meet a lot of nice people over there, I suppose."

"Come on, man. Get off it. She's not gonna stay there. Just until this thing with her daddy wanting to shoot her blows over."

"It might not just blow over, Leon. She might not be able to come back." He got up from his seat. "I got some work to do. Hey, kid, you can stay here if you want. Hang out; get to know the people. Just be home before dawn, okay?"

"Yeah," Rufus said, "okay. Sure. Whatever."

"We are concerned for him," his brother said quietly when the door slammed shut and Rick was gone.

"Yeah," Rufus said, "I'm real worried myself. I've never seen him act like this."

"His first wife died tragically," Alex said. "She died of cancer. He lost her too soon. Now he worries he may lose someone again."

139

"He's gotta snap out of it," Leon said, pulling the computer back to him. "Hey, what's this? Oh my God! What is this?" He was now looking at the screen that displayed the latest news, sports, and entertainment.

"What is it?" Alex asked, sounding bored, and finally emptying his glass.

"Isn't this guy that girl's father?" Once again he turned the computer around. "Look. This guy here. Augustus James Rivers the Third. The rich billionaire bastard who fracks all over the place and poisons all the drinking water."

Rufus leaned over so he could see. "Yeah, that's the guy she says is her dad. Only he's not her real dad, she found out. He's the one who hired the hit man." And he read the screen. "The FBI is after him now? How come?"

Leon clicked to open the article. "It says here someone has been mass mailing all kinds of papers, some on his personal letterhead. Someone's been sending them to the FBI, the EPA, and major newspapers and stuff." He continued to read, "Oh, sheesh, look at this—one of them is a photocopy of a handwritten note. It's dated for the same date one of his factories blew up, it says, 'one hundred thousand to take care of labor relations problem.' Oh man. This looks like it's gonna be big."

"I wonder who could have done it," Alex said. "It can't be what's-her-name, because according to what I've been told she's been too busy dodging bullets."

Rufus swiftly stood up. "We gotta go tell Rick."

Leon and Alex got up and followed him out the door.

Rick couldn't believe what he was hearing. "You did what?"

The old woman stood there before him, "Yes! I did it. And now I need a place to hide!"

He had arrived at the front entrance of his gallery to see Zelda standing there waiting for him, and so he let her in. As soon as the door was shut, she began talking excitedly. He had difficulty following half of what she said since she was in such an excited state. He listened and finally figured out what she was trying to tell him; and so then he led her upstairs so she could take a seat in his living room on the couch where Rufus slept. She continued on and on.

He sat in a soft chair opposite her and waited for her to finally pause. "Wait a minute. You are trying to tell me that you gathered up evidence against him for years? And now, after all this time, you are sending it around everywhere? If you had evidence that he was involved with crimes, why didn't you go to the authorities right away?"

"Because I wanted to stay there, as long as I could, to watch over my granddaughter. That's why! That fool always thought I could not speak English, or maybe he thought I could not even read. So he had me clean up his office, nobody else. I pretended to be stupid, and watched her grow up. She ran away, so then I made my move while he's away on a business trip. But now I hear he's coming back early. He might suspect it was me. And now I need a place to hide, because suddenly I am very, very scared!"

"Well, Zelda, someone shot out the front window to my place, so this isn't a good place to hide," he said. Plus, it wouldn't be good for her to look into his refrigerator one morning while looking for cream to put in her coffee.

"Maybe I can stay at Laura's place. You must have a key?" she asked.

In fact he did not have a key, but he said, "That's not a good place, either. She was being watched. Let me think about this a minute." His brother was a landlord who had a few small apartments that were currently empty. "This will only be until the FBI picks him up, right? You know, a man like Rivers will just deny everything. I'm sorry, Zelda, but maybe you didn't think this through. You've put yourself in a lot of danger by doing this. You say no one else cleans his office, so naturally now he'll think that maybe you can read English after all. I just have to find a place for you to hide out until we see what happens with this guy, if he gets arrested or not. He could probably just buy his way out of trouble and get away with everything like he always does."

She listened to him silently and then startled when there was a knock at the front door that led into the gallery downstairs.

"I'll see who it is. And I hope it's not one of his henchmen." He got up to go downstairs to open the door. On the way down he swore to himself, wondering what the hell the old woman had gotten herself into. He reached the door and saw it was Alex, Leon, and Rufus. Leon and Rufus looked all worked up. Alex appeared slightly annoyed, like he always did during a crisis.

"What?" Rick asked.

Leon and Rufus rushed in, and Alex followed slowly.

"Rick!" Leon said. "Listen, it's all over the internet!"

"What's all over the internet? Somebody's cat tossing a hairball on a rug?"

"Rick!" Rufus barked. "Someone is sending all kinds of incriminating documents about your girlfriend's evil rich-ass father who's not her father anymore. Leon saw it on his computer. It might even be on TV."

"Oh. That. I already know all about it."

"Has it been on the news?" his brother asked, and then added, "But I suppose you see things online sooner than on the television these days."

"No. I haven't turned on the TV. You guys come on upstairs." And then he called out, "Zelda, it's okay. These are people who can keep a secret, okay?"

When they entered the living room Rick repeated, "These guys can keep a secret. Okay? I know they can." He introduced them, "This is my half-brother Alex. This is my friend Leon, whom I think of as a brother. And I think maybe you might have met Rufus? And they can keep a secret."

Zelda looked at Rick and smirked, "What kind of secrets would such a nice man like you have?"

Rick looked at her and said nothing, even though three of the people in the room were vampires, and that was enough of a secret to keep. "Okay, guys, this is Laura's grandmother Zelda. She is going to need a place to hide for a while. Because she's just gotten through telling me all about the evidence against Rivers that's been sent everywhere."

Laura woke up and first noticed that she felt slightly cold. She opened her eyes and rolled to look toward the window. There was a light dusting of snow on the branches of a tree outside, but yet she could hear a bird weakly singing, as if spring was trying to arrive but it was not quite there yet. The sun, also, was bright and strong; the sky did not look like it still belonged to winter.

She sat up, and looked at her diamond-studded watch. It was early afternoon. She must have slept quite a long time. She did not recall what time she fell into bed the night before, but she knew it was extremely late, nearly close to the time when Rick and his friends and relatives would sleep.

She looked around the room and was struck by how old fashioned it looked. There was a round multi-colored braided rug on the floor; it appeared hand crafted. The furniture was simple, dark wood and sturdy, from another era. She was covered with an old and slightly faded handmade patchwork quilt.

Laura suddenly also realized she had slept in her clothes, and that she wasn't exactly certain where she was right now. "Whose house is this?" she wondered. Slowly things came back to her. She followed behind another car last night. It was driven by a lady named Josephine ... yes, that's right, she told herself. And she was to stay at this house while she was in town. And that was about all she could remember.

She found her purse on the floor beside the bed and pulled out her mirror. She reacted with horror when she saw what she looked like: makeup in disarray, her previously neat hair had gone running amok. She hoped the apparently ancient home had a functional bathroom so she could shower and wash her hair and get herself together before meeting anyone, if that was what she was to do.

An hour later she wandered downstairs, hair slightly damp but presentable, and hoping to find a kitchen that was stocked with something other than the blood of cattle. She let herself down the slightly darkened staircase, and then down a dimly lit hallway, and headed toward where she could see light. As she got closer she smelled coffee. She emerged into a tidy but out of date kitchen with appliances that appeared to be decades old yet functional.

"Hi!" There at the old heavy wooden table was a young woman with blonde curls, sipping coffee and reading a small town newspaper. She seemed familiar to Laura somehow, as if she should recognize her.

"Hi," Laura said cautiously.

"You're the lady who's staying here for a few days. I made you some coffee. There's a box of donuts on the countertop next to the stove."

"Thank you," she said. "That's wonderful. I really need some coffee right now. And I must say, you do have a very lovely old home. I'm Laura," she introduced herself, and then she caught herself almost saying Laura Rivers, "Laura Blasko."

"I know," the girl said simply. "I'm Sharona. I rent a room upstairs, down the hall from yours. I don't own the house. The lady who owns the house isn't home right now. She's going to college full time. She'll be back. Her name is Muriel." Sharona got a mug from the cabinet and poured Laura a cup of coffee and got cream out of the refrigerator for her also.

Laura sat down and inhaled the steam. "Thank you," she said again, and added a small amount of cream to her coffee. She didn't know what to talk about. She certainly couldn't say that she was in town to deliver a small package from one vampiress to another, since she was not certain how much this girl knew about the situation. The owner of the home must not be nocturnal, she guessed, since she was out and about during the day. "Well, it's rather unusual to see snow in spring, isn't it?"

"No. This time of year, the rain comes and washes away the snow, but then you get a cold day and some flurries, and get a little snow like this. It looks like winter all over again. But it will all be gone soon. Then the flowers will come out, and the leaves will be back on the trees, and the geese will return to the lake. It's just like the endless cycle of death and rebirth, and the way that time moves in a circular pattern."

Laura was surprised that someone so young seemed so philosophical. "I guess you could put it that way."

"And speaking of Mother Nature, have you heard the news?"

"Why no," Laura said, "I haven't kept up with the news. I've been travelling."

"It looks like they finally got something on Mr. Pollute the Rivers, something that will stick to him like the sludge he dumps into the drinking water." Sharona pushed the newspaper toward Laura. "If it interests you. You must know who I'm talking about, right?" She smiled.

She reached to take the newspaper. "Oh my God."

Augustus Rivers sat at his desk, speechless with cold hard rage. His secretary left messages that the FBI wanted to speak with him. He told her to say he was out of town, but soon they would probably come for him.

145

He would have to buy his way out of it again. It was the cost of doing business.

Where was that worthless old cleaning woman? The mystery of whether or not she could read English might have finally been solved. And now it was going to be a problem. He would deny everything, of course, and say it was a hoax perpetrated by environmentalists who just wanted to stop progress. It would cause some difficulties for a while, but it would go away in time, like all his other problems did over the decades. He had always found ways to deal with his problems.

The phone on his desk rang. "Hello?" He listened. "She's stopped running? Good. Take care of it. I don't care if she's staying with other people. Just make it look like a burglary or something. Take care of it, Vito. And when you're done, I'll have another job immediately after. Get it done! I'm sick of waiting for a resolution to this problem. I don't care who else gets in the way. Just do it!"

He slammed the phone down. He smiled to himself, leaned back and put his feet up on his desk. It would be taken care of. And the rest of his problems would be cleared up. It was only a matter of time. And money. Judges could be bought. And so could federal agents.

As evening slowly approached Laura realized it was close to the time that she was to meet with this vampiress named Annasophia and deliver the small box, as she had agreed. She repeated the name over and over in her mind, thinking of what a romantic and exotic sounding name it was. She wondered if she were beautiful and glamorous like Irina, who routinely wore multiple diamond and ruby bracelets with matching necklaces and long diamond earrings cascading down to flash from behind her raven dark hair.

She had brought one good outfit with her to wear, to appear presentable. If Rick were with her she knew he'd wear the same thing he wore to the art exhibit, again.

She missed him, and when she thought of what she read in the newspaper she hoped the FBI would hurry up and take Augustus Rivers to prison, so she could go home and get on with her life. It was the first time in her life she felt happy; she had friends, people who cared about her, and was finally beginning to feel as if she belonged somewhere. And now the man she once believed was her father was set to ruin it all for her again. She wished They, whoever They were, the federal government, the powers that be, would hurry up and take him away. Then the man who was pursuing her would probably give up, forget about her, and go look somewhere else for "work," she hoped. But then she worried Mr. Rivers would just buy his way out of trouble . . . again.

She went through the small bag she had packed mostly casual clothes in, and pulled out the black silk pants that she got recently from a high end boutique, a pale pink satin blouse, the string of pearls which were her mother's, and Italian kidskin heels. She wrapped a pale pink scarf around her neck and wore the pearls around it. Even though she was familiar with vampires, she preferred that her personal life not be that obvious, as she still bore a small scare from the last time she was with Rick.

And then finally she remembered the gift. She reached into her purse and found the small box wrapped in ornate gold paper. She wondered what it could be. She would feel ridiculous if she got ready and went to meet people and forgot to bring the package with her.

And it finally dawned on her that she felt awkward, and was probably going to feel even more awkward as the night went on, because she was about to meet people she had never met before, and spend time with them while attempting at meaningful conversation. In addition, the people she was about to meet were vampires. She had known vampires before, of course; but the ones she already knew were friends and family of Rick. She wished he were here to make sarcastic comments to make her smile. "Would they be as nice as Rick's people?" she wondered. Officially she had arrived to bring their greetings along with a small gift; but truly, she was on the run from a hit man.

There was a cautious rapping at the door to her room. "Come in."

It was a dark haired young woman of medium height, in slightly faded blue jeans and a long sleeved mauve cotton shirt. She appeared to be somewhere in her twenties, Laura guessed.

"Hi," she said. "I'm sorry I didn't meet you before, but you came in so late the other night, and, well, I hope you've been comfortable."

"You must be Muriel." Laura smiled and put her purse down on the bed. "I've been wanting to tell you what a beautiful old house you have, and to thank you for your kindness in letting me stay here."

"Oh, well, the old house is a lot of work," Muriel said, "but thank you. I inherited it. It's a project, really. But I suppose it could be in worse shape. They say you've come all the way from the west coast?"

"Yes, and it was very long and exhausting trip. I've been staying in hotels along the way, and they were not all that comfortable, either. They told me I should get on a plane, and now I wish I did, but," she hesitated, and thought of an excuse, "maybe I wanted the adventure of taking a long road trip."

"That's a nice car you have out there," Muriel said. "You don't see many like that in this little town."

Laura was slightly embarrassed. "Thank you. It's actually the first car I've ever owned."

"Really?" Muriel looked back almost in disbelief. "Most people, their first car is an old Chevy." Then she laughed. "But

148

maybe things are different in California. Come on downstairs. Sharona brought some fried chicken and a blueberry pie from the place where she waitresses and we can all share."

Laura followed as Muriel descended the stairs. "I've never been in a home with such character and charm." She had in fact been in all sorts of homes, but most of them were mansions that were somewhat newly constructed, or older mansions that were professionally renovated. She had never actually set foot inside an old house that was sort of a "project" like this one was. She went downstairs and took it all in, the wallpaper old and slightly faded but in decent condition, various paintings on the wall apparently from the Victorian era, the dark wood paneling that looked old but cared for, and the furniture, old and slightly dusty but not too badly worn or used.

"The wallpaper was coming off in some places," Muriel admitted when she noticed Laura looking around. "But I actually very carefully glued it back up and hopefully it will stay where it is now. It hasn't fallen down since, and most people don't seem to notice unless they really stare at it. The furniture was here when I arrived, and most of it is in good enough shape. For a Victorian, it's not really that big. But it's big enough to rent rooms out to people, which I plan to do. You know, a boarding house."

Sharona was in the kitchen already digging hungrily into the container of fried chicken. She looked up and cheerfully said, "Hi."

Muriel got some plates from the shelves and put the kettle on the stove to brew some tea.

"So," Muriel began when they all sat down, "Laura, I guess you're going out to meet some people tonight?"

Laura hesitated. "Yes, I guess that's right."

"I think Josie is coming to pick you up," Muriel said. "Oh, yeah, I should tell you, Sharona knows these people, and I know these people; but . . . it's something they like to be quiet about.

I mean, not everybody in this whole town knows about, you know, stuff. You probably realize that already."

"I understand," Laura said quietly. "Actually, I wasn't certain how much you two knew about these people I'm going to meet tonight. And truthfully, ladies, I feel a bit awkward and apprehensive. I mean, I know people like this back in California, and they're very nice, but well, it's probably just because I don't know—"

"They're very nice, too," Muriel said. "When I found out, I couldn't believe it myself, at first. But, well, yeah," she laughed quietly. "Oh well, they exist, and they're here. And that's that."

Laura wondered if the vampires she would soon meet knew the true purpose of her visit. Perhaps she would be less welcome if they knew she was actually hiding out from a hit man. That was part of why she felt awkward. And what would she say when she got there? What would they talk about?

Suddenly Sharona looked up from her plate and dropped the drumstick down. She gazed straight ahead, her eyes glazed over, and she appeared to be looking at nothing. "Excuse me," she whispered. She got up from the table quietly.

Laura heard her footsteps softly going upstairs. "Is she okay?"

Muriel hesitated, "I don't know. I hope so. I hope it's not the chicken."

"I hope not," Laura said. "I'd hate to go out tonight and try to make a good impression and get sick all over the place. That wouldn't look too good."

There was a sudden knock at the door, not a soft tapping sound but a pounding, as if someone were demanding to be let in.

"It's kind of early for Josie," Muriel said. "I'll see who this is." She got up to answer the front door.

Laura reached for another chicken wing while looking over the blueberry pie. Suddenly she noticed a small grease stain on

150

her blouse. "Oh no." She hoped no one would notice. That wouldn't make a very good impression either. For most of her young life, she had been taught the importance of appearances . . .

"Oh my God! Oh my God! Oh my God! Don't point that gun at me!"

It was Muriel. She had answered the front door. And Laura knew right away she had been tracked down and found.

"What do you want? Money? We don't have any money. I have some old silverware. You can take that. Get that gun out of my face, okay?"

"Shut up."

It was a man's voice, not loud, but cold. Dead cold.

And then Laura heard what sounded like the snarling of a fierce dog. She fought the overwhelming urge to find a closet to hide in. Instead she got up and looked cautiously around the corner and down the hallway that led toward the front entrance. There, standing between Muriel and the intruder, was a large silver-furred dog—or was it a wolf? Ears back, fur raised, and with a growl that echoed strangely, as if the sound came not from the animal, but from out of the air itself. And she noticed something else. The wolf seemed translucent somehow, not quite solid. She could almost see through it, as if it was a ghost wolf. But how was that possible?

She blinked and took her eyes away from the wolf and looked up to get a better look at the intruder. Middle aged, slightly graying hair, expensive looking leather jacket. She recognized him. She did not know his name, but she had seen him before when he came to the mansion, most likely to discuss a job or to collect payment. She knew Mr. Rivers always paid cash for certain jobs.

But then she looked again at the wolf. Where did it come from? She had never seen it or any animal in the house. Had she seen it before? Maybe she had. In her dreams?

151

The man pointed his small gun down and aimed to shoot the wolf. Muriel turned to run. Multiple gunshots. The wolf continued to snarl.

"Die you stupid dog!"

More gunshots.

Muriel came running toward her. "Call 911!"

Laura hurried back to the kitchen to reach for the old rotary phone on the wall. She dialed. Nothing.

"Oh my God. I think the phone is dead." Instantly Laura knew the man must have cut the lines outside the house.

"Damn it!" Muriel shouted. "My cell phone is in my car!"

More gunshots.

"My phone is upstairs, in my purse," Laura said, sounding at the edge of panic. "And I would have to go back through the hallway to get to the stairs."

They heard the man in the front entranceway complain, "Why the hell won't this stupid animal just die?"

Another long drawn out snarl.

"Run out the back door! Come on!" Muriel said. "Let's get outta here!"

Laura followed Muriel out the back door. They ran down the back steps. But then she felt herself suddenly yanked by her hair and then painfully dragged back into the kitchen.

"I'm out of bullets," he said without emotion, "but I can still break your neck."

She heard Muriel come back into the house. "Get the hell off her!"

"Muriel!" she screamed. "Run! Save yourself!"

He threw her down on the floor and leaned over her. Laura felt cold hands grip her throat. She dug her nails into his flesh, but he didn't let go. She tried pulling his hands off, but she wasn't strong enough. And then, she felt couldn't breathe. She felt the pain of her throat being crushed. Then all was darkness.

Next she heard a thud, and suddenly she was released. She coughed and choked, breathing rapidly. She rolled over, moving away from the man, reaching up to grasp her throat.

"You bitch!" But this time he was talking to Muriel.

Laura opened her eyes and looked up. Muriel was standing over the man with a large, heavy wooden rolling pin. "It came with the house," she said.

He knelt on the floor. She raised it again to slam down on his head. But he was too fast. He got up and reached to snatch it from her grip.

"Now I'm just gonna have to kill the both of you! Not that I wouldn't, anyway." Slowly he stood up with the rolling pin to advance toward Muriel.

Laura struggled to stand. She reached for the rolling pin and tried to pull it out of his hand. He simply shoved her back down to the floor. She got up again, and seeing he was coming toward Muriel with the rolling pin aimed at her head, she jumped on his back, wrapping her arms around his neck as tightly as she could.

"What the hell are you trying to do, you crazy broad?" he said, almost laughing. "Come on, will yah? Just make my job easy! I'm getting too old for this. I just need a few more jobs and then I can retire." He swung around with Laura still clinging to him, making her legs slam against the thick, heavy wooden kitchen table. He spun around again to shake her loose and she landed on the floor. She saw him leaning over her and she quickly began to crawl away.

"Leave her alone and get the hell out of my house!" It was Muriel. She was going through the drawers under the kitchen countertop, searching . . .

And Muriel now had a knife.

"What's that, honey?" he said. "You got a little kitchen knife? Real cute." He dropped the rolling pin and reached into his pocket and took out a switchblade. "Only I got one better than that."

Laura looked at the switchblade and continued to struggle to get away. Before he could once again get a grip on her, she got up to run. But as soon as she stood up, she saw Sharona standing there, where the hallway opened into the kitchen. She wore a gray fur over her head; it covered her shoulders, and went down her back. She looked pale and cold and silent, her eyes glazed over, as if she was there and yet looking at something that no one else could see.

"Oh man, you crazy broads in this house are gonna make my job difficult. Now I gotta kill all three of you dumb bitches."

Sharona drifted slowly forward, looking as if she was in some sort of trancelike state, advancing toward him.

"What? You wanna die first? Okay, fine."

She came closer and swiftly took hold of the hand that held the switchblade before he could use it on her and with her other hand reached to press against his forehead. The man then appeared to fall into a seizure. He froze and let out an almost inhuman cry of horror, *"Nnnnnooooooooo!"*

He dropped the switchblade and fell forward to land on the floor on his knees. Burying his face in his hands, now sobbing like a frightened child. Muriel put her small kitchen knife down on the countertop and came to snatch up the switchblade. "Oh my God. Sharona, what did you do to him?"

Sharona turned to Muriel and said quietly, "I let him see what I can see. He is surrounded by the spirits of all the countless lives he's destroyed, and they number in the hundreds. Men, women, children. People shot, stabbed, strangled, burned, poisoned, blown up. Their souls follow him wherever he goes, and I made him see them, to look into their eyes, and see what he has done. I made him see the horror he has caused, and see the lives he cut short in this world. I let him feel their sadness, and hear their cries, and know their endless pain."

Laura now stood away from him, her back against the wall. Her blouse was torn, and she still felt the pain in her throat as well as pain from the impact against the kitchen table. She stared down at him in terror, expecting him to rise up again and come for her, even though he continued to sob into his quivering hands—hands that had almost choked the life out of her. She now also noticed that her head hurt from when he had yanked her by the hair. She then looked at Sharona, her head still covered with the pelt, wolf ears sticking straight up, tail touching the floor. *"W-what are you?"*

It was Muriel who tried to answer, "Well, Laura, you already know that vampires aren't like what you see in the movies. Right? Well, werewolves aren't like you see in the movies, either. They don't physically change into wolves. It's kind of like they leave their body, go into the form of a wolf, and talk to ghosts, and—"

"Muriel," Sharona said, "let's explain all that later and tie this fool up."

Muriel pulled out the long wire that connected the rotary phone to the wall and handed it to Sharona.

"Oh my God." It was Josie, suddenly coming into the kitchen from the front hallway. "Muriel, I saw your front door was wide open. I walked in and saw there's a gun on the floor over there! And there's bullet holes all over the floor. Who is this guy? You got a burglar?"

"N-no," Laura confessed. "I have to apologize. This is my fault. My father . . . no . . . I mean, the man I used to believe was my father, he sent this man to kill me. I thought if I came here, he would never find me. I almost go you killed, too, Muriel. I feel so horrible about this. I have no idea how he found me here. I am so sorry! I hope you'll all be able to forgive me."

Josie only half listened; she continued to stare at the man curled up on the floor, almost now in a fetal position. He continued to sob quietly while Muriel tightened the telephone line and secured his wrists behind his back, *"Make them go away,"* he cried. *"Send them away. I don't want to see them anymore. Make them go away!"*

"He found you because he put a tracking device under the rear bumper of your car," Sharona said. "I saw it when I looked into his mind."

"What?" And then Laura remembered seeing someone standing near her BMW when she watched Rick leave the parking lot outside her apartment. She jumped when she heard the teakettle begin to whistle.

"But why would your father want to kill you?" Muriel asked, pulling the wire tight and tying it as securely as possible. She had forgotten about the kettle being on the stove during the disturbance, and went to shut it off as soon as she felt the intruder was tied up well enough and would not get loose.

Laura hesitated and then tried to answer. "I'm not completely sure myself, but maybe he doesn't like to leave loose ends, or maybe he sees me as a mistake that should never have happened. I don't know. You see," Laura continued, clutching her bruised throat and realizing that her pearls had fallen off and landed on the floor somewhere, "for most of my life, I believed Augustus James Rivers was my father. He always hated me, and I never knew why." A tear slowly drifted down her cheek, but she swiftly brushed it away. "He always told me terrible things about myself, that I was incompetent and not good for anything. I could never make him proud of me." She continued to tell her story, trying to be heard over the man's continued mumbling and sobbing. "Finally one day I left home, hoping he'd never find me. When I left, I had a lot of trouble adjusting to life in the real world. I couldn't drive. I couldn't cook. I didn't even know how to do my own laundry. I had trouble making friends because, well, I'm rather shy. I felt stupid and useless, and started to think he was right, that I was no good for anything. I guess you would say I had very low self-esteem. I even started to think about taking my own life. I realize now that Mr. Rivers brought me up to hate myself. Then I met someone, and well . . . he was a vampire. How I found out about him would take too long to tell, but I actually asked him to kill me. But he wouldn't. He made me realize I didn't have to be perfect to be good enough, and that I don't have to live up to anyone else's expectations but my own. He was happy with the way he was, even though he's different. He made me realize that it was okay for me to just be myself. It was like a weight was lifted off of me. After a while, I realized for the first time in my life I was happy, and felt loved. And then, I found out that Mr. Rivers is not even my real father. But he still wants to kill me. That's why he sent this man. And I also know that Mr. Rivers has had other people killed before. I can't prove it, but I think he has. I've seen this man at my father's . . . I mean, at Mr. River's mansion, once or twice. I don't know his name, but he always frightened me whenever I saw him."

Finally the hit man quieted down slightly, but continued to mumble almost in a whisper, "I don't want to see them . . ."

"This man has done a lot of work for Mr. Rivers," Sharona said. "And for others, also. He's killed for money, many times: for Rivers, for the mafia, for drug lords. He kills for money."

Muriel took off the leather belt from her blue jeans to tie his ankles in case he came to his senses and tried to run.

"Maybe you should gag him, too," Josie said. "He just won't shut up. It's really annoying."

"Josie," Muriel said, "do you have your cell phone? Call Karl."

Sharona bent toward the hit man's ear and said directly to him, "You are going to write up a confession and you are going sign it. Because if you do not, you will go directly to that place

157

you call Hell. You are going to tell everything so that the world will know all the evil that Rivers has done. And then this girl can finally be free."

Sharona sat in a small chair next to Sergeant Stepanek's desk at the small police station, her wolf pelt now wrapped around her shoulders like a fur stole, as if to keep warm. Karl was typing the document on his computer and complained, "How many more pages is this going to go on for?"

Vito Roselli was now in handcuffs, sitting opposite Sharona, and therefore he could not write the confession himself as he had been ordered to. Instead, he dictated it. He gazed down at the floor, mumbling on and on about his vast multitude of crimes. As the night went on it had been discovered that he had five different types of identification in his possession with five different aliases, but Vito Roselli was his real name. He had been killing people for a living since he was in his early twenties, and had started his career as an enforcer for the mob. After the FBI had rounded up most of those that he had worked for, he began to work for anyone who needed to get a job done quietly and efficiently. He had done a lot of work for Augustus James Rivers over the years, including blowing up the factory where about two hundred lives were lost and killing off many of the people that had filed a lawsuit against Rivers Industries to stop fracking near their farmland, in addition to various other jobs he had performed. Finally he admitted to causing the brakes to fail on the car driven by Laura's mother. Vito was good at making things look like accidents, which was one of the reasons why Mr. Rivers hired him so often. Several different types of military assault rifles and assorted ammunition were found in the trunk of his Audi along with a machete; however, he only took one gun with him when he went in to do this job.

"You went into the house with one small gun and a switchblade to finish this job you were supposed to do?" Karl asked coldly. "I would think an experienced professional like yourself would have gone in better prepared."

"It was just a couple of women. I figured it would be easy."

Sharona snarled like a wolf, eyes wild and baring her teeth. Vito cringed.

The sergeant reached for the mug next to his computer and took a sip. When he did, he spilled a small amount of blood. It dripped onto the desk, making a small red stain.

"What the hell kind of people are you in this town?" Vito suddenly shrieked. "This crazy girl here is growling at me like a wild animal, there's a dog back in that house that disappears into thin air when I try to shoot it, and what the hell is that you are drinking?"

"Calm down, Vito. This is not about us. This is about you. I'm going to lock you up and when the day shift comes in I'm going to have them to call the FBI to come and collect you first thing in the morning. They will most likely interview you a second time. And if you know what's good for you, you will leave out the part about the wolf."

"That was a wolf?"

"I appeared as a wolf in front of him so Muriel could get away," Sharona explained to the sergeant. "He emptied his gun trying to shoot me, you know, trying to shoot the wolf. But the bullets just went into the floor."

"What?" Vito said.

"Be quiet," Karl said with preternatural calm. "We're asking the questions, not you."

But Sharona continued to explain while gazing vacantly at Vito, "When he ran out of bullets, I just dematerialized, and then came downstairs myself to see what else I could do to stop him. I saw that he was surrounded by the spirits of all those he killed. His presence made the room really spiritually crowded. I've never seen so many ghosts in one place. There was so much energy around him I was able to use it against him and I made him see what I saw. I made him see the tormented souls that follow him everywhere; and there were so many of them, I could not count them all. I hope they can all be at peace now, when justice is finally done." She then looked directly at the sergeant. "These things were meant to happen. This is how the universe balances itself. Evil can go on for a long time and cause a lot of damage, but eventually spiritual forces that are at work will cause it to be stopped."

"I'll have to leave that part out of the report," Karl sighed. He looked down on the surface of his desk and gazed at the small tracking device he had pulled from under the BMW; it had been cleverly attached with an adhesive. It was evidence, along with the gun and the switchblade and other assorted items found in Vito's possession. Karl then leaned back and put his feet on his desk, picked up his mug and took another sip. "I suppose it's like being a cop. We're outnumbered. There are just a few of us against wife beaters and molesters and drug dealers and all kinds of assorted trash. But we don't give up, and there's only so much we can do. But eventually, we catch up with them and put a stop to whatever they're doing."

"That's right," she agreed. "Evil is everywhere. But every act of goodness, every act of kindness, no matter how small, keeps this world from going over the edge into oblivion."

"What the hell is this crazy broad talking about?" the hit man mumbled, as if forgetting that several hours ago he could not get the terrible vision of the multitude of tormented souls out of his mind.

"That's enough, Vito," Karl said coldly. "She's not the one going to prison. That's you and Rivers both."

Josephine helped to carry an old braided rug up from the basement of the old house and into the hallway so Muriel could cover up the bullet holes. She then left to tell Sophie about all the trouble and that Laura probably wouldn't be meeting with them tonight. Josie sighed and gave Laura a cold look before going out the door.

Muriel found Laura's pearls on the kitchen floor where the struggle with the intruder had taken place. She expected that all the pearls would have fallen off the string to roll away, but when she picked them up she saw that the string was knotted between each pearl, so that even though the string was broken, none of the pearls had gone missing. She held them in her hand and saw they appeared to be genuine and of a good quality, "These must be yours," she said, and handed them to Laura.

Laura sat at the kitchen table, leaning forward, her face in her hands, and still shaking. She looked up briefly and whispered, "Oh. Thank you."

Muriel observed that she still looked upset and frightened.

"He'll be locked away tonight. You won't have to worry."

"I know . . . I'm just . . . I guess I'm just still in a state of shock." And then she blurted out, "Oh Muriel, I'm just so sorry about all of this! You could have been killed because of me."

"You said you didn't know he was following you?" Muriel was skeptical, and there was an edge in her voice. Did Laura come here to visit and bring a gift from far away? Or did she come and stay in her home just to hide from a killer? Then she recalled the police sergeant reaching under the BMW to pull the tracking device out from under the rear bumper. It was small, and she had never seen anything like it before. In fact, she didn't realize such things existed until now.

Laura looked directly at Muriel and said, "He tried to kill me twice back home in California. We thought he might be tracking me through my cell phone. So I gave up my cell phone and my friends gave me another one. It wasn't my idea, really. The lady who sent the gift, she has an adopted son. I kind of think he's the one who thought it up, that I should come here. So I don't think it was her idea, really. They were going to order plane tickets to send me out here, but I told them I didn't want to get on the plane, in case the assassin knew I was getting on it. I actually worried that if I boarded a plane it might blow up in the air with all the people onboard. Mr. Rivers might actually arrange for something like that to happen. He blew up one of his own factories because of a labor dispute. So I insisted I would drive across country to get here, just to avoid getting on a plane and endangering everyone else. I only learned to drive about a year ago, believe it or not. I was afraid to go across country all alone, but I felt I had to. Besides, since I thought maybe he was tracking me through my cell phone, maybe he was listening in, too, and might have overheard the conversation about getting plane tickets. I don't really know much about these things, this tapping into people's phones. I'm not that technological. But I thought maybe it might be possible. So instead I drove all the way. It was exhausting. And I was so sure I wasn't being followed. But now I know how he found me." She sunk down again, face in the palms of her hands. "Oh Muriel, I've really messed things up."

"What do you mean, messed up? You just said you didn't think he'd follow you out here." Muriel pulled out a chair and sat beside her.

"Don't you see how awfully bad this is going to look?" Laura said, at the edge of tears again. "Why, I was supposed to be bringing a gift from the vampires on the west coast to the vampires out here. And I still don't know what is in the box. The way I heard it, they only just recently started communicating. They didn't know about each other before. This is going to really look bad, not just for me, but for them. I really messed this up. This wasn't supposed to happen like this. My mistake in driving out all the way here will make them look bad. Don't you think?"

"I don't know," Muriel sighed. "I honestly don't know how they're going to feel about it."

"Maybe I should have gotten on the plane. I was so stupid, Muriel."

"But what if you were right? What if he did hack into your phone?"

"Do you think someone could do that?"

"I'm not that technological, either. But now they say the government can do it, so if the government can do it, why can't a hired killer with the right kind of equipment? I really don't know. But what if you did get on the plane, and it blew up in the air? All those people's lives would be lost, just like you said." Muriel realized now that even though there were bullet holes in her floor, her kitchen was a mess, and she was herself badly shaken up, no one had died that night. If it were not for Sharona, they might both be dead right now.

"And oh my God, Muriel," Laura suddenly looked up again, eyes wide, "I just realized something."

"What?"

"Didn't you say that girl was . . . *a werewolf?*"

They talked for many hours until they both fell into exhaustion and could say no more.

Sharona finally drifted through the front door of Muriel's house, exhausted, the wolf pelt still wrapped around her shoulders like a shawl. There was a light on in the kitchen, and so she headed in that direction.

"Oh, you're back," Muriel said and sleepily looked up at her. She was now in her blue plaid flannel pajamas and sitting at the kitchen table with an empty teacup and a small plate of crumbs leftover from the slice of pie she had eaten. "I went to bed but I just couldn't sleep, not after all that craziness that went on."

"I know," Sharona said. "I don't know if I'll sleep too well either now." She was still trying to clear her head of the memory of seeing the dark cloud of spirits that surrounded the assassin as he made his sudden and violent entrance. The sight of hundreds of them, clustered about like a dark vapor with their sad and tragic faces floating through the murk, all of them crying out in unison for justice and an end to their pain. Sharona had seen troubled spirits before, but not so many at once. Vito had carried them all with him, everywhere he went, without seeing them or knowing of their presence, until tonight.

"Hey, Sharona," Muriel said. "Listen, you saved our lives. If you weren't here—"

"I know." She sounded as tired as she really was. "It's what I do," she said, brushing it off as if it was nothing. "Yeah, lucky it was my night off from work, too." And she knew there were no coincidences. She sat down, and then asked, "How is she?"

"Laura? She finally went to bed, but she was awfully upset. She went on and on. Her childhood, she could never do anything right, her father the billionaire, only now he's not her father, so now he wants to kill her, she was never allowed any friends growing up, and now her only friends are vampires and a few other people she knows. And now she thinks she's irreparably harmed the relationship between two groups of vampires, or something. Oh, and now she knows you're a werewolf. Sorry."

Sharona put her head down on the wooden table, feeling weak from exhaustion. "Oh well. Yeah. Okay. It's not really your fault she knows. She saw me. I mean, she saw the wolf, in the hallway."

"Do you think things will be okay?" Muriel asked, "I mean . . . ?"

"She had a tough time in life, I think." Sharona got up to go upstairs to bed. "But about the other thing she's worried about now, I don't know how it will turn out. I'm so tired, I just can't think about anything right now." She slowly dragged herself upstairs. The house was quiet. The spirits were gone—to their final rest, she hoped—except for the one that inhabited the home, but he was quiet also.

Josephine hardly noticed that Sophie's home had been cleaned up and reorganized since the last time she had visited. She was so upset with what had occurred that she did not notice that the entire house had been put in order; that the shelves and even the antique trinkets and picture frames that were on the shelves had all been cleaned and dusted. All of the bolts of fabric and ribbon and even the sewing machines were stashed away, resulting in an almost shocking neatness. Instead of noticing the difference, Josephine sat on the couch with her purse on her lap and continued on about it bitterly while Sophie patiently listened, ". . . Oh my God, and there were bullet holes in the floor when I came, too. I don't like it one bit, Sophie." Her voiced was almost shrill. "Muriel could have gotten killed. They should never have sent that girl here!"

Sophie sat opposite her in a soft and slightly worn out chair, a delicate teacup in her pale hand. "We were aware that she was travelling because she had some sort of trouble at home."

"We didn't know that trouble meant a hit man that would follow her out here."

"Well, you did say that Karl pulled some sort of device out from under her car," Sophie sighed and added, "Well, is the trouble over now?"

"How can you be so calm about this, Sophie?"

"Josephine," she answered quietly, "for over two centuries I have seen all sorts of mayhem and destruction, usually perpetrated by the ignorant, naturally. My own family, those I love, my dear Ben, the list goes on. Now I will ask you this, who died tonight?"

"Well . . . No one."

"And so then, what did we lose?"

Josie was almost silenced by Sophie's logic. "Nothing, but—"

"I think we can be sure that none of this disaster was intentional, Josie."

"Well—"

"And I will tell you something else." Sophie put the teacup down and pointed a long thin white finger directly at her. "For over two centuries I have lived with the sadness of thinking we were all alone here in this small town. I have often many nights, when no customers came into my dress shop, stared despairingly out the front window, looking up into the night sky before closing up, and looked out and wondered if there were any others like us, somewhere, out there, under that same dark sky. And now, finally, we have found others of our kind, even though so far away. Do you not realize how important this is to all of us, Josie? And we simply cannot afford to lose contact with them now, after centuries have gone by. This is very important, no matter what mistakes have been made."

Leon returned home after work, tired but not yet ready to sleep. He was used to working nights. It was early dawn and he decided to check his computer for messages. It had been a while since they had heard from their new contact on the other side of the country. Rufus told him that Rick was still worried since there had not been any other messages since Laura's arrival.

He clicked to open his email and hoped for an update, or anything new.

"Oh my God," he said out loud.

The house where Laura was staying had been broken into by an armed man. Apparently he had found her by attaching some kind of electronic device to her car. The man was now in custody. The police in the small town would be contacting the feds to pick him up, and this man had a lot to tell. He read on.

You told us she had a thug problem. You didn't tell us she had a problem with a professional thug. She says her crazy father sent him. Thanx, man.

"Oh, shit."

He looked around frantically for his cell phone. It was somewhere in his small and untidy apartment. He kept looking

166

until he located it between the cushions of the cheap old couch he watched TV on and ate on and sometimes slept on, "Hello? Rick?"

There was no answer. Maybe he was already asleep.

"Damn it." He threw the phone down. It bounced off the cheap couch and landed on the never vacuumed shag rug. "Damn it," he said again. It was his idea to send her all the way across country, after all. He thought she would be safe there, and the hit man would eventually give up trying for her, he hoped. And then she could come home.

But it didn't work out the way he planned it. He had tried to be the hero. Instead, he had let everyone down.

"Oh shit, I really messed it up." He looked down and gazed at the rug that covered the floor beneath his feet. When he bought it Alexandra said it was an ugly shade of burnt orange, and now, suddenly in his misery, he realized she was right. He also realized that when Irina found out that the killer had followed Laura all the way out to the East Coast, she'd be royally pissed. And so would Rick, even more so. He picked up the phone again and dialed Alexandra. She did not answer either. It was too late for any of them to answer.

Hastily he clicked Reply and began to type back, *OMG, so sorry. We thought that guy would never find her way out there. She okay?*

"Damn it," he repeated as he shut the computer off.

The first thing Laura became aware of was the sound of the songbird in the tree outside the window. Slowly she opened her eyes and saw the brightness of the late morning sun. Or was it early afternoon? She wasn't sure. Then she recalled the events of last night. She also became aware of the pain from all the bruises she had gotten in the scuffle. Her face was still stained from dried tears. She knew that if she looked under her satin nightgown she would see multiple spots of black and blue along with some red. She tried to sit up but it hurt to move. She noticed her throat still hurt as well.

Was he really gone? She wondered. Was the man who tried to murder her last night finally locked away in a cold steel and gray concrete cell where he could trouble her no more? And what of Mr. Rivers? The man she once believed was her father? Did they—the government, the police, or whatever entities exist to ensure that there is justice in this world—finally catch up with him, also?

She slowly and painfully forced herself to get up enough to look out the window. It was a bright new day. The bird was still chirping. She looked out and saw leaves just starting to appear on the trees outside, a sign of early spring.

She then remembered her conversation with Muriel that had continued until late last night. The neighborhood was populated with vampires who arrived from Eastern Europe to escape persecution over a century ago. They owned a lot of the local farms, and got blood from dairy cattle. And now she was aware there was a werewolf renting a room in this same house, just down the hall. Not a werewolf like in the movies, but a sort of psychic shapeshifting person that Muriel had a little more trouble explaining.

Oh well, she sighed. It wasn't that much different from back home.

But what if she had in fact really messed things up? Was Mr. Rivers right after all? Was she really that useless?

She tried to stop herself from thinking like that. That kind of thinking had almost led her to do away with herself once. She had believed everything that Mr. Rivers had told her since she was a small child. But now she knew he wasn't even her real father, and she knew that he was responsible for her mother's death, and for her real father's death, in addition to his many other crimes.

And the hit man Mr. Rivers hired had followed her all the way across country without her realizing it. It wouldn't look good for her. And it wouldn't look good for the vampires on the west coast, either. It would look like they had sent her travelling across country along with her troubles. But she had agreed to go and she needed to face whatever problems she had created alone now.

And then she heard a light tapping on the door. It couldn't be the hit man. He was supposedly locked away. She slowly went to open the door. It was Sharona.

"Oh, hi," Laura said weakly.

Sharona's lustrous blonde hair was slightly damp from the shower and she was dressed for a normal day in faded and almost threadbare jeans, black long sleeved t-shirt and faded denim vest. She seemed bright and awake despite last night's horrific adventure. "There's coffee downstairs," she said.

"Okay," Laura answered. "I guess I'll get dressed and come on down." She quietly shut the door and put on her jeans and sweatshirt and combed out her hair before making her way down to the kitchen. Pausing to gaze in the mirror that was above the bureau, she realized she was now almost used to her new dark-haired appearance. On the way toward the staircase she looked briefly into Sharona's room as the door was left half open. It was neatly kept, with few personal possessions. It appeared the girl owned only her clothes and the large wolf pelt, which was now spread out over the bed like a fur blanket.

On descending the stairs she not only smelled coffee but also bacon. When she came into the kitchen she looked around warily and saw that there was no assassin lurking in any dark corner. The table was set for two.

"Muriel is at class this morning," Sharona said. She seemed cheerful despite the events of the night before. "I usually work nights, so I can sleep late."

Laura found a mug and helped herself to some coffee, "About last night . . . I mean . . . I don't really understand a lot about what you did. But thank you."

"It had to be done. He had to be stopped. People like that need to be stopped. And he needed to be made to see what was following him, to see what he had done with his life," she sighed while frying the eggs and bacon. She pointed at the chrome toaster on the countertop by the coffee brewer. There were already four slices of white bread in it. "Why don't you put the toast down?"

"Okay."

"You know, Laura, the world is full of people like that. They cause a lot of suffering, but they always come to their own destruction in the end."

"I think I'm beginning to see that now." She only hoped that the destruction would eventually reach all the way to Mr. Rivers. She leaned against the countertop and sipped her coffee, "So . . . I guess you're a . . ."

"Yeah. I know," she answered casually. "Shapeshifter. Werewolf. Whatever."

Laura liked to consider herself open minded toward paranormal creatures. She continued to sip her coffee and listened.

Sharona continued, "It was passed down and taught in my family. There used to be a lot of us." The eggs were done and she shut off the stove. She got a large fork and a spatula and put the eggs and bacon on the plates. "People like us used to be able to do a lot of good, until around five hundred years ago. Then things changed. People turned on us, and hunted us down the way they hunted down the witches. They hunted down vampires, too. But I never knew any vampires until I came here. People like us, we have to live in secret now. I really don't know if there are any other werewolves besides me left in this world now."

The toast popped up. Laura found the butter already on the table and put the toast on the plates.

They sat down to eat and Sharona kept talking, "I don't know why the world is the way it is now. Thousands of years ago, there was peace on Earth. People and animals lived in peace. People talked to the spirit world all the time. That's probably around the time my ancestors got the wolf spirit that followed my family down through all the ages. That's what a lot of people did then; they would ask the spirit world for a guardian to come to them. Sometimes it was an animal, like a wolf. Animals have spirits, too, but most people just don't know it. Sometimes spirits attach themselves to a family, like the wolf spirit that came to my ancestors, way back in history. But never mind. Anyway, hundreds of years, maybe thousands of years go by, then things changed. No one knows why. Now there is war all over everywhere. Pollution, poverty, homelessness. They are destroying the forest and dumping poison into the water. The spirits watch over the world and try to influence people to stand up and change things back to the way things should be, but it's hard because not enough people will listen. Most people just listen to their own greed."

"Maybe greed is the problem, then," Laura sighed. She didn't understand a lot of what Sharona was saying, but found it interesting. And she knew all about people living under the influence of pure greed and had grown up surrounded by opulence, cold selfishness, and pure greed.

But Sharona continued on while she cut up her fried eggs, "People who help the homeless, peace activists, people who work to save animals, those are the ones the spirits are able to influence."

Laura nibbled delicately at her toast and wondered, though, about the world being so saturated with evil. "Aren't there bad spirits, also?"

"Sure there are," Sharona said with certainty. "They can work their way into a person's head, too."

She then thought about the man that she had long believed to be her father, and she wondered if he were influenced by strange forces in some way. Then suddenly Laura recalled that after she had literally run away from home and found a safe place to live, she encountered a self-proclaimed psychic who claimed that he was from a higher realm. "Back home," she began slowly, "I mean, where I came from, there was this odd character who used to say he was a messenger of some sort, and he said that he was from a higher realm. But he charged a lot of money. I think he turned out to be an out of work actor, or something."

"There are a lot of dishonest people who say they can do these things." Sharona continued to eat hungrily, like a wolf. "If someone charges a lot of money, don't pay any attention to him. It's best to just listen to what you think is the little voice inside telling you what is the right thing to do. Because if you can't actually see spirits or hear them clearly and speak to them, well then, that's how you can listen to them."

"I see," she sighed, and finished off her coffee. She started on the eggs and eyed the bacon. "Well, Sharona, I just really hope I didn't ruin things by coming here."

"By coming here, the man who was sent to kill you was captured. He talked all night long about working for Mr. Rivers, and all the terrible things he's done. Now the world will know. Mr. Rivers won't be able to hide behind his money anymore."

"I do hope you're right."

They finished breakfast. Sharona washed the dishes in the sink and Laura found a dishtowel and helped to dry them so that Muriel would not come home to find the kitchen in disarray. After a while they sat together on the back step that faced the small backyard and talked. Laura told Sharona about her childhood, and Sharona told about hers. Laura could not imagine growing up in a small and simple home with few material things besides what was necessary. She again explained what her early life had been, growing up surrounded by cold hearted opulence, her existence controlled by a man who did not love her, who mercilessly criticized everything about her and who made her feel unwanted, unloved, and useless; until one day she ran away and found she had difficulty coping with the real world, also. She didn't realize how sheltered she was, and didn't even know how to drive a car until about a year ago. She came close to taking her own life at one time. After finally finding some happiness in life and a place where she felt she could belong, the man she had believed to be her father sent someone out to kill her.

Laura listened to Sharona's story and after a while she realized that they had some things in common. They were both orphans. They were both suddenly on their own. And they had both suddenly found themselves among new friends and having to start life over. Sharona told her that her life had been mostly happy until disaster took away her grandparents, "But we still talk sometimes," she said. "I just don't see them that often now. I think maybe they're getting ready to finally move on to the higher place."

Laura tried to understand as Sharona went on to explain, "This world we live in, everything we see, that's only the physical world. There's another world, the spirit world. They don't need money or private jets over there. They watch over us and try to guide us from where they are. They're all around us. We don't always see them or hear them. But they're there."

Laura sat and silently wondered about her mother and real father, and wondered if they watched over her. She hoped they did, and hoped she would meet them someday. She listened while Sharona continued to talk while gazing at the trees at the edge of the forest.

It dawned on her that as the hours passed by, the time would come when she would be once again expected to meet with people—with vampires—that she did not know and had never met before. She would need to compose herself and hope they wouldn't be angry with her for bringing her troubles with her.

Josephine did not speak much as she drove Laura down the dark forested road that led to Annasophia's house. Laura weakly attempted to make conversation, but Josie just gave simple one word answers if she spoke at all. She seemed cold, where she had been friendly and talkative when they had first met.

Laura wanted to ask Josie if they could ever forgive her, but she kept silent. She wished that Sharona could have come with her, but she had to work. Muriel could not go with her, either, even though she said that she would want to come. She had a night class she needed to attend.

Finally they arrived. Laura got out of the car and saw the small house hidden behind a row of trees. There appeared to be a light on in only one room. She reached into her purse once again to reassure herself she did not forget to bring the small package. Whatever was in it, she did not know. She hoped that her appearance was acceptable. She once again wore her silk scarf, but now to hide the multitude of bruises she received during the attempt to kill her. Muriel had lent her a simple pink sweater to wear, as her expensive blouse had been torn and was beyond repair.

The front door swung open without Josephine knocking. A beautiful woman's face appeared from out of the dim light. "Come in. Please, come in! You must be Laura. And it's so good to finally meet you."

Laura hesitated, "Thank you, I—"

"Come in," she insisted.

Josephine turned away and said, "I need to get to work."

"Okay, thank you for driving me." Laura didn't expect a reply, and there was none.

"I thought this was your night off, Josephine, dear," the woman called after her. "Never mind. Come on," she said again to Laura, "we've been waiting for you."

She went inside and when her eyes adjusted she saw an attractive woman in a simple white silk blouse and dark brown long woolen skirt. Her dark blonde hair was arranged with tortoiseshell side combs, simple and old fashioned yet elegant. She was not at all like Irina, who radiated wealth, sophistication, and glamour.

"Come this way, please." The woman beckoned her to follow her down a dark hallway. At the end of the hall was a small well-lit room. When she arrived she saw there were people already there. She hesitated before entering and eyed the people—vampires—who were there waiting for her. Then she immediately recognized one of them. It was the policeman who took the hit man away in handcuffs as he continued to mumble about seeing all the ghosts of the many people he had killed over the years. He was in uniform, and she was surprised to see him there. She realized she should have known he was a vampire the first time she saw him due to his fair complexion, but she had experienced so much trauma that night that she couldn't pay much attention to anything besides her own pain and terror.

He stood up to greet her, extending his pale yet strong hand, "Nice to see you again, Miss."

She took his hand, "Oh. Hello, I—"

"I can't stay long," he said. "I need to get back on the road. I just wanted to be sure you were all right."

"Yes," she said, "thank you. I'm still a little shaken, actually. But I think I'm going to be all right."

"I see you've already met Karl," the blonde woman said.

"Yes. Yes, we've met." Laura didn't mention how deeply embarrassed she was as to how they had met.

Karl continued down the hallway. "Glad to see you're okay," he said. He turned to say to the others, "I've got to go, see you all later." And then he left.

"Let me introduce you to the others that are here. This is Elton." She gestured to a dark haired man sitting quietly in the corner, away from the single lamp that lit the room. He looked up and acknowledged her silently. "And this is Seymour."

Seymour sat on the other side of the small room. He looked up and said hello so quietly she almost didn't hear him.

"Of course there are many others of our kind in this area. But Elton and Seymour are also friends of Muriel. You see, it is because of Muriel that we have been able to finally locate others of our kind, after so long not knowing if there were any of us left in this world. And oh," she continued, "I am Annasophia. But please, just call me Sophie."

Laura looked around and made an effort to smile and be pleasant. "Thank you. Well, it's very nice to finally meet you all."

"Please, do sit down," Sophie said.

She sat in a soft chair and noticed that on the small table in the center of the room was a pot of tea, a few delicate teacups, and a small plate of biscuits. She guessed they were set out just for her, as the others most likely had no interest.

"Oh," she began, "I just remembered. I'm supposed to give this to you." She reached into her purse.

"Please, gifts are not necessary." Sophie sat on the smaller chair that was right beside hers. "It is enough that we know there are others of our kind in this world and to receive their greetings." But she accepted the small box that was handed to her. She slowly opened it, carefully as if trying to salvage the colorful wrapping paper.

Finally the box was opened. Sophie was speechless and so was Laura. The diamond necklace flashed before their eyes. Everyone stared in amazement.

"It must be worth a fortune," Seymour commented.

"Maybe that's why they didn't want it sent in the mail," Elton said.

Laura looked in their direction and said, "I really didn't know what was in the box. I had no idea."

"I brought much jewelry with me when we came here from the old country so long ago," Sophie said as she put the necklace on and then found the matching earrings in the box. "But sadly I sold most of it when times were hard. This is very beautiful, Laura. I will give you something to take with you when you return. But now, please, tell us all about those of our kind that you have come to be acquainted with in faraway California. We must know all about them."

"Well," she inhaled and began shyly, "they came to this country around the time of the Russian Revolution."

Laura returned to Muriel's house very late that night. Elton gave her a ride back and he came in to say hello to Muriel but Sharona told him that Muriel had already gone to bed, and so Laura thanked him for the ride and he left. She stared after him almost longingly as he went out the door.

"He reminds me of someone back home," she said to Sharona. "Someone that I miss very much."

"So, how'd it go?" Sharona asked.

Laura smiled with relief. "Better than I thought it would, really. That lady seems very nice, and so did the other two. The policeman was there, but he did not stay long. She—Sophie, I mean—she wants to give me something to bring back with me when I go. And they want to exchange addresses and emails, and to start corresponding across the distance, to keep in communication, and such. She said this is the first time in over a century they've heard from any others of their kind."

"I found a newspaper left on a table that I was clearing at work," Sharona said, changing the subject. "The FBI wants to talk to Mr. Rivers. That man who came here, the feds have him now. They came and took him away."

"Good." She sighed with relief and said, "I think I'm just going to get on a plane to get home as quickly as possible, and arrange to have my car transported back to California by truck. I know that can be done because Mr. Rivers would have his cars delivered wherever he wanted that way. It took me so long to drive across county. It was an adventure, but I'm just too tired to ever want to do it again. And if the FBI wants to talk to me, I'll leave my address and phone number at the police station for them to get in touch when I'm home. I'll be glad to tell them everything I know. But right now, I just want to go home." Laura suddenly drew Sharona close in a quick embrace. "And if it wasn't for you, I wouldn't be able to get home. I'd be dead."

Laura looked up into the semi-darkened sky above and watched the jet plane drift by overhead. It headed west, toward home. But she looked around and found herself on the ground. Under her feet she saw the rough grass that made up the small backyard behind Muriel's house, and directly ahead was the forest. She didn't know why but she headed into the woods, into the darkness surrounded by the seemingly endless trees. She found a pathway and followed it, not knowing where it led her. And then out from behind the trees appeared a shadowy gray wolf. It stopped directly in front of her.

"Oh," she said, slightly startled. Should she turn and run? Or was she dreaming again? Then the wolf was gone. Instead, Sharona stood before her.

"Life is a journey," she said. "We don't always know where we're going, but it doesn't matter as long as we arrive at the right place."

The forest around her, the trees, the sky above, and everything suddenly faded away. She awoke with a start and opened her eyes and realized she was on the plane heading for home. Slowly she remembered her sad good-byes to Muriel and Sharona. Even Josephine came over to visit the night before she was to leave, and so Laura knew that she was no longer angry with her. She was now filled with the memory of an adventure that was so unbelievable that she almost wondered if she might have dreamed it all.

As her head cleared she realized that perhaps Sharona was right. Some things were meant to happen after all. Because of a chain of events and things she did that she believed were just foolish mistakes, justice was going to finally be done. Were there really forces at work? Were there really influences from outside of the material world that helped to bring about change? She didn't know, but she expected that the moment she arrived home the FBI would want to talk to her. She also felt she should speak with the tabloid reporter that Rick knew. It would be safe now, she supposed, to finally let the truth out. But she could only tell what she knew about Mr. Rivers, his crimes, and the one he hired to perpetrate those crimes on his behalf. She would just need to leave out the part about the shapeshifter who talked to spirits.

Suddenly she got up from her seat and opened the overhead storage compartment. There above she saw the beautiful handmade quilt that Sophie asked her to bring back for Irina. Next to it was the sketchpad that she had brought with her when she left home. She took it back to her seat with her and pulled a set of pencils from her purse and began to draw. It would be hours before she would be finally home.

Rick gazed down at her in the semi-darkness and looked over the bruises. She had briefly explained before finally falling asleep in his arms. But before she did, he said the man who did it was lucky to be in jail, where he could not get at him.

As soon as he woke up that evening, he got a call from Leon telling him that he had borrowed Irina's car to pick Laura up at the airport, and that she was finally home. Rick told Rufus to watch the store and got into his old Pontiac and went to see her. When she opened the door he saw the black and blue. "Who the hell did that? I'll kick his ass."

She let him in and she told him she was exhausted, but went on about her adventures, "I feel like I've been all the way to the moon and back."

She showed him the beautiful handcrafted quilt that was to be given to Irina. "But first," she said, "I just need to get some sleep. I still hurt all over from someone trying to kill me, again." She went on to tell him she wanted to talk to the reporter that he knew after all, and that the FBI might be wanting to talk to her, too. She was ready now, she said. It was time to let the world know the truth about Mr. Rivers, and that she was alive, despite all his efforts.

She fell asleep with him beside her, and while listening to the quiet drone of the television, hoping to catch a snippet of information. Hours later, getting close to dawn, she stirred awake when it was announced that Augustus Rivers had disappeared, that federal agents went to his mansion and found he was gone. Computers were seized, and staff were being questioned.

"I hope my grandmother will be okay," she mumbled, sounding half asleep.

"Where do you think he's gone?" he asked when he saw her eyes suddenly snap open on hearing the name of the man who had tormented her for most of her young life.

She was still in his embrace when she sat up. He released her and she reached for the TV control and turned the volume up. "I don't know. He has houses everywhere, Europe, South America, the Bahamas, he has places where he could go. He probably took one of his cars to the airport and got on his private jet before the FBI could catch up with him. He probably left as soon as he realized they had Vito in custody and that he was going to talk."

"Vito?"

"The hit man," she yawned. "That's his name. Vito Roselli. He's the one who tried to shoot me twice but missed. Then he followed me all the way across country, and tried to kill me out there. But he didn't."

He got up off the bed. It would be time for him to go soon. "What are you going to do now?"

"Just live my life. I'm not going to let him cast his shadow over me anymore. Now he'll be the one in hiding, or on the run. Maybe he'll finally forget about trying to kill me."

He looked down and saw her sketchpad on the floor next to the bed. He picked it up and flipped through it. There he saw a pencil sketch of a young girl, wearing worn out jeans and a t-shirt, and with a wolf pelt covering her head and going down her back. It was just a simple drawing, but there was something about it that made him not want to stop looking at it.

"It looks like you had an interesting time," he said.

"There are so many amazing things to tell, and I don't even know if I believe half of it myself."

The full moon's silver light brightened the night sky and shone through the trees of the vast pine forest. The night was alive with the sounds of the crickets and the cool but gentle wind that brought the fragrance of early spring with it. It had been a long time since she walked these woods, enjoying the quiet and the dark of night. She remembered wandering through forests like this over a century ago, in the old country. The cool scent of the whispering pines brought back so many memories, some happy, and some sad.

And then, off in the distance, she heard the long, drawn out howl. She continued to walk on.

Annasophia had heard the talk from customers that visited her shop bringing their repairs and alterations before she closed up for the night. The people in the small town were whispering now that in the forest prowled a wolf, and so she knew that the spectral wolf could be seen by both those in the spirit world and the living alike. She walked on, hoping to catch a glimpse, hoping to find Sharona when no one else was close by.

There, from behind a centuries old fir tree, emerged the gray shadow-like form, so deeply gray to almost be black, almost as dark as the night itself.

"There you are," she said, and she gathered herself. "I need to ask this of you. I know you will see him again. I know that in your travels on the other side you will once again come across the one I love. Tell him for me . . . tell him that I still love him, and that I will never love another, no matter how long it is that I am on this earth, tell him I will only love him."

The wolf stared back at her and quietly whimpered.

"I know that the cruel pain you feel inside will cease over the years," she said, "but sadness never really goes away when you lose someone."